Ralph Keeler

Vagabond Adventures

Ralph Keeler

Vagabond Adventures

ISBN/EAN: 9783337178680

Printed in Europe, USA, Canada, Australia, Japan

Cover: Foto ©Andreas Hilbeck / pixelio.de

More available books at **www.hansebooks.com**

VAGABOND ADVENTURES.

BY

RALPH KEELER.

BOSTON:
JAMES R. OSGOOD AND COMPANY,
Late Ticknor & Fields, and Fields, Osgood, & Co.
1872.

TO

𝔐𝔶 𝔬𝔩𝔡 𝔉𝔯𝔦𝔢𝔫𝔡

EDWARD P. BASSETT, Esq.,

This book is affectionately inscribed, with the wish, which is hardly a hope, that the public may take my Life half as easily and good-naturedly as he takes his own.

R. K.

CONTENTS.

——◆——

BOOK I.

AMONG WHARVES AND CABINS.

Æt. 11.

BOOK II.

THREE YEARS AS A NEGRO-MINSTREL.

ÆT. 12-15.

Contents. vii

BOOK III.

THE TOUR OF EUROPE FOR $181 IN CURRENCY.

ÆT. 20–22.

Contents.

CHAPTER III.

CHAPTER IV.

CHAPTER V.

BOOK I.

———◆———

AMONG WHARVES AND CABINS.

Æt. 11.

CHAPTER I.

IT is an odd sort of fortune to have lived an out-of-the-way or adventurous life. There is always a temptation to tell of it, and not always a reasonable surety that others share the interest in it of the *conteur* himself. It would, indeed, be a nice problem in the descriptive geometry of narrative to determine the exact point where the lines of the two interests meet, — that of the narrator and that of the people who have to endure the narration. I cannot say that I ever hope to solve this problem ; and in the present instance, especially, I would with due respect submit its solution to the acuter intellects of others.

This little book is intended to contain a plain sketch of my personal history up to the close of my twenty-second year. The autobiographical form is used, not because of any supposed interest of the public in the writer himself, but because there does not seem to be any other way in which a connected account of the adventures can well be given.

No one, I think, can be more sensible than I am that my story is nothing if not true. Hume has wisely said, "A man cannot speak long of himself without vanity." I should like to be allowed to add that I have never known or conceived of a person — except probably the reader and writer of these pages — who could talk five minutes about himself without — lying. That is, to be sure, reducing the thing to mathematical exactness. An overestimating smile, or an underestimating shrug of the shoulders, or a tone of the voice even, will always — though sometimes inadvertently —

> "leave it still unsaid in part,
> Or say it in too great excess."

While this is not so applicable to written history, still in the face of hyperbolic and bathetic possibilities I owe it to myself to premise that I am going to be more than ordinarily truthful in this autobiography.

And there is certainly some merit in telling the truth, for it is hard work when one is his

own hero, and not what is sometimes termed a
moral hero at that. I can too, I may add, claim
this single merit from the start, with a meekness
almost bordering on honesty ; since it happens
that I am forced to be veracious by the fact that
there are scores of people yet in the prime of
life who are cognizant of the main events of the
ensuing narrative.

CHAPTER II.

FAMILY MATTERS.

IT may be laid down as a general principle, to start with, that a boy had better not run away from home. Good and pious reasons are not wanting, and might be here adduced, in substantiation of this general principle. Some trite moralizing might be done just now, in a grave statement that an urchin needs not run away into the world after its troubles, since they will come running to him soon enough, and that a home is the last fortress weary men build (and oftentimes place in their wives' names) against the slings and arrows of outrageous misfortune. Why, therefore, it may be asked, with overwhelming conviction to the adult, — who, by the way, is not supposed to be one of the congregation of the present preaching, — why, therefore, should the juvenile fugitive hasten unduly to leave what all the effort of his after life will be to regain?

Thus having done my duty by any boy of a restless disposition who may chance to read these memoirs and be influenced by my vagrant example, I proceed to state that I ran away from home at the mature age of eleven, and have not been back, to stay over night, from that remote period to this present writing.

It is due, however, to both of us, — the home and myself, — to observe that it was not a very attractive hearth that I ran from. My father and mother were dead, and no brothers or sisters of mine were there, — nothing at all, indeed, like affection, but something very much like its opposite. On the whole, I think, under exactly the same circumstances, I would run away again.

But I hope this remark will not lead the thoughtless reader to assume that I am not of a respectable family ; no well-regulated memoir could be written without one. A "respectable family" has long since become the acknowledged starting-point, and not unfrequently the scapegoat, of your conventional autobiography. *A posteriori*, therefore, our respectability is established from the very fact that there is an autobiographer in the family.

When, however, a great truth has once been discovered, it is always easy to find many paths of proof converging toward it. When Kepler, for instance, by some strange guess or inspiration, hit upon the colossal fact that the planets move in elliptical orbits, it was comparatively an easy thing, — or should have been, to make this scientific parallel correct, — to come at half a dozen proofs of it in the simple properties of the conic sections. Thus, too, fortunately for us, the respectability of our family can be proved in many ways, and even, like Kepler's Laws, by mathematics itself. Nay, our proofs can be, and indeed are, established by common arithmetical notation and numeration ; because the members of our family are generally rich.

This is manifestly an unusual advantage for an autobiographer, since, as is well known, he almost invariably comes of "poor but honest parents." And there is no little pride mixed with the candor with which I boast, that I am to this day, pecuniarily, the poorest of my race.

The devious course of my wanderings, as a youthful negro-minstrel and as the European tourist of one hundred and eighty-one paper dol-

lars, left me in the early part of my life no time
or inclination to look into such commonplaces as
the matters of my inheritance. It was but a
week ago that I rode over the broad Ohio prairie
where I was born, and passed by the pleasant
farms which, with the broad prairie, were the pat-
rimony left to me, — or, I should say, to the kind
gentlemen who administered them for me. That
property has never been any care to me. It was
so thoroughly administered during my minority
that I have never since had the trouble even of
collecting rents.

Now there may be people, of a recklessly imaginative type, who suppose it would excite a
pleasurable thrill to ride thus over a great prairie
which bears one's own name, but no more tan-
gible emolument for the quondam heir ; and there
may be people of so aspiring mental constitutions
as to think it a grateful, rollicking piece of vanity
to pass unrecognized through a town which was
once sold by one's own administrator for fifty-two
dollars : but I am free to confess that I have
endured these honors within the past week, and
have carried nothing away with me, in the matter
of gratification or sentiment, but a dash of the

sadness which has settled about the wreck and ruin of the old homestead.

Nothing seems to thrive there but the cold-spring at the foot of the sand-ridge, and the poplar and weeping-willow which grow above it. These trees had and have for me a plaintive undertone to the rhythm of their rustling leaves which I do not hope to make others hear. The willow was the whip with which a friend rode twenty miles from the county-seat to visit my father, in the early times, and it was stuck in the ground there, on the margin of the spring, by my little sister ; the poplar was planted beside it by my mother. They are both tall trees now, and a sprig from one of them has been growing a long time over the graves of father, mother, and sister.

At an early stage of my existence and of my orphanage I was introduced to a species of *in transitu* life, being passed from one natural guardian to another very much as wood is loaded upon Mississippi steamboats. It was, indeed, rather a rough passage of short stages, — each, however, more remote from my Ohio birthplace ;

and I have always thought there would not have been so many figurative slivers left behind in the hands through which I passed, if the passage had not been so rough and headlong. Finally, at the age of eight or nine years, I was shipped away to Buffalo, N. Y., to be placed at school.

I was sent thither down Lake Erie from Toledo, on board the old steamer Indiana, Captain Appleby commanding. Many are yet living, I suppose, who will remember this craft, — the first of the kind upon which I ever embarked. For my part, at least, I think I shall forget everything else before I forget the noble sheet-iron Indian who stood astride of her solitary smoke-stack, and bent his bow and pointed his arrow at the lake breezes. A meagre brass-band, too, as was the generous custom of those days, was attached to the steamer, and discoursed thin, gratuitous music during the voyage. To a more sophisticated gaze the attenuated, besmoked brave of my juvenile rapture would, alas! have looked more like an indifferent silhouette plastered belligerently against the sky; but it was the first piece of statuary I ever saw, as that execrable brass band made the first concert I ever

heard, and the Apollo Belvedere, at Rome, or
Strauss's own orchestra, led by himself, at Vienna,
has never since excited in me such honest thrills
of admiration. It was many and many a month
before that swarthy sheet-iron Indian ceased
occasionally to sail at night through a mingled
cloud of coal-smoke and brass music, in my
boyish dreams.

The lake was remarkably calm, and the entire
passage to Buffalo was for years one of my pleas-
antest memories. On that first voyage, undoubtedly, was engendered the early love of steamboats, the fruit of which ripened soon afterward
into the adventures I am about to relate. Nothing, I am convinced, but this boundless affection
for the species of craft in question enables me to
remember, as shall be seen directly, the names of
all the old lake steamers I had to do with in my
boyhood.

And this, by the way, is no small internal evidence of the truth of what follows. But I should
not have called your attention to the fact, and I
should not have been forced to parade my con-
scientiousness here again, if I had not come
already to the most embarrassing period in all
my history.

Without seeming to manifest a feeling which I am sure I do not now entertain, I cannot write about the two or three miserable years I passed in Buffalo ; and, if I omit to write about them, a great share of the dramatic flavor of my story is lost. I cannot, therefore, convey to you even the regret with which I am compelled to pass over this period of my life, because you cannot know, as I think I do, that exactly such a childish experience of unlovely restraint has never yet got into literature.

Every time I pass the old Public School-house No. 7, in Buffalo, I stop and gaze at it with a queer sort of interest. Yet I cannot confess to any sentimental regard for it ; since it was, after a manner, the innocent cause of my enduring, at least, the last six months of my unpleasant life in its neighborhood. If I had not been so interested by day in the Principal and duties of that school, I am sure I should have fled much sooner than I did from the roof which sheltered me of nights.

Finally, however, one domestic misunderstanding, greater than many others, brought me to a

conclusion which was certainly as comprehensive in its wrath as it may have been lacking in a
premise or two of its logic. At this temperate remove from that exciting period I am led, at least,
to doubt — in the interest of certain kin of mine,
who could hardly have been responsible for facts
they knew not of — whether I was not guilty of
that poetic fallacy, placed in its first utterance, I
believe, in the mouth of an illustrious Trojan, and
worn very threadbare ever since in the mouth
and practice of almost every one, — whether I did
not, that is, learn a great deal too much from one
to judge very unjustly of all.

At any rate, in the domestic crisis just alluded
to, I rebelled against authority whose insignia were
fasces of disagreeable beech-whips, and, at the
mature age of eleven years, took a solemn vow
that I would have nothing more to do with the
people of my home circle in Buffalo, or with any
whatsoever of my relatives, some of whom had
placed me there ; — and I ran away.

CHAPTER III.

ESCAPING from the house at night, I did not have time or presence of mind to take anything with me but what I carried on my back.

One of my school-fellows, who had been forewarned of my design, met me by appointment on the neighboring corner, and smuggled me into his father's stable. Here, it had been agreed, I was to lodge on the hay.

My friend was a doughty, reassuring sort of hero, who was a great comfort to me at that nervous moment when I entered the darkness of the hay-mow. I would not for the world have betrayed any fraction of the fear which his swaggering manner may have failed to dispel. He would assuredly have laughed at me ; and I believe now, moreover, he would have taken that, or any shadow of an excuse, for joining me in my flight.

So strong, indeed, was the romantic instinct

upon that young gentleman that he lingered long
about the spot where I had crawled into the hay
and covered up my head, before he could prevail
upon himself to go back to the house and to his
regular bed.   He had assured me before we came
into the stable, out of the pleasant moonlight of
that late spring evening, that he envied me very
much, as I was going to have lots of fun ; he only
wished he had a good reason to run away from
home too ; but then, he added thoughtfully, as he
looked up at the lights in the window of the family sitting-room, his mother was so "*derned* kind,"
and his father so "*blamed* good," that he did n't
see how he could leave them just now.

The next morning my friend found me sleeping
very comfortably, with my head and one arm protruding limply out of the hay.   Awaking me, he
proceeded to draw from his trousers pocket several pieces of bread-and-butter for my breakfast ;
which was none the less toothsome from its somewhat dishevelled state, consequent upon the manner of its previous stowage.

While munching that surreptitious meal, my
thoughts very naturally wandered to the breakfast-
table, where I should that morning probably be

missed for the first time by the people from whom
I had fled; and I amused myself, as well as my
romantic caterer, with what we both of us, no
doubt, considered a highly humorous account of
the grievous commotion which would ensue at
that ordinarily so solemn victualling.

Emboldened by the lively appreciation of my
school-fellow, and by the reviving influence of the
bread-and-butter, I grew imaginative and grotesque in my daring pleasantry. I went so far as
to describe the scene at that breakfast-table when
Bridget came to the dining-room door with wild
eyes, and the announcement that my room had
not been occupied on the night before; how the
pater-familias, at that dramatic moment, had
dropped a surprised spoon into the splattering
gravy of the stewed meat; and how his wife opposite, then in the act of pouring chiccory, had —
whether in dismay at the overwhelming news or
at the sudden soiling of her tablecloth — upset
the coffee-pot.

These and many more very brilliant and mirth-
provoking feats of boyish humor — very brilliant
and mirth-provoking, of course, I mean, to my
friend and myself — did I perform that morning

2

in the hay-mow; all bearing upon the assumed
utter discomfiture of the bereaved people about
that breakfast-table. But, alas! even a precocious
autobiographer, with his mouth full of bread-and-
butter, may make the mistake, so common to the
adult of his species, of over-estimating his own
importance. I have since learned that there was
no sensation of any consequence at the breakfast-
table in question, and that my subsequent permanent loss was taken with remarkable equanimity
and resignation.

It was an expressive, nay, eloquent, look of
envy and admiration that my friend gave me,
when it came time for him to leave me to my own
devices for the forenoon, while he went reluctant-
ly to school. Even to this moment I cannot say
that I covet the amount of knowledge he carried
away from his books that day, or, indeed, the
succeeding three days.

I sallied stealthily forth to amuse myself in the
by-streets till he came back at noon to bring my
dinner; which consisted of a repetition of the
breakfast, with the added dessert of an apple.
This latter he carried carefully in his hand, but
the bread-and-butter he invariably bore stowed

away in his trousers pocket; I say invariably, for I lived two or three days thus on his secret bounty.

About dusk of the second evening he came to me with — in addition to the bread-and-butter for my supper — the startling news, that he was going to take me to the theatre. I do not remember how we got in, — it was not, certainly, by paying our way. I incline to the opinion that my friend had some secret understanding with the door-tender. I know merely that, by some means, we achieved our entrance to the pit of the old Eagle Street Theatre.

I have heard good citizens of Buffalo complain that, since Lola Montez burned down that seat of the histrionic Muse, the drama has languished in their city. Of course I am not competent to decide in such matters; but, that being the first playhouse of any kind I ever entered, I am glad to be able to say that I have never since seen anything in the theatrical line so absorbingly thrilling, or so gorgeously magnificent, as the old Eagle Street Theatre was to me that night. The name and plot of the play I have forgotten; but the dark frown of that smooth villain in the third act — where his villany first began to show itself to my unpractised comprehension — will never fade from my remembrance.

I do not know how it was, but up to that time I recollect I was under the juvenile impression that virtue and correct grammar always went together. I can therefore convey no idea of the shock with which I learned so late in the play, that the splendidly dressed man who could talk such eloquent, persuasive language, and withal in such scrupulous conformity to that most difficult of rules which keeps the verb under the regimental discipline of its subject-nominative, — that the man whose plaintive periods sometimes rose to the iambic majesty of blank verse, and who never got a case or tense wrong, howsoever wild, ecstatic, or dithyrambic his utterances of devotion to that innocent, long-suffering angel, the walking-lady, — that this man, I say, should nevertheless turn out to be a monster, whom, to borrow a little from his style of phraseology, it were mild flattery to call the greatest and vilest of rogues.

My memory of the whole evening is swallowed up in the overwhelming shock of that sad surprise. The grammatical Arcadia of my boyish belief was laid waste as with an earthquake.

The next morning, after I had eaten my usual bread-and-butter with more than usual appetite, I received a few choice friends at my lodgings in the hay-mow, and we had a consultation.

It was suggested that I was too near my former haunts to be safe. Indeed, rumors of an actual search for me had reached the ears of one boy, of whom, oddly enough, I can recall nothing more now than that those ears of his were remarkably large ones, and stood out prominently from each side of his head; that the best and most picturesque view of those ears was, in my opinion, to be had from my desk just behind him at school; and that I was especially attracted and edified by my observations upon them immediately after he had had his hair clipped short.

Those are grotesque pranks, by the way, which the memory sometimes plays us when we attempt to grope back too far. Another one of those daring spirits, for instance, who was loudest, and therefore, I fear, most influential, with his coun-

sels that morning in the hay-mow has faded, as
to body, name, and station, wholly from my mind,
and exists to me now literally as a cherub with
a mammoth straw hat for wings. From anything
that I can positively remember, I would not be
prepared to take my oath that he ever had any
arms, legs, or trunk at all. I can recall only his
big, round, staring eyes, which stood out at the
tops of his puffy cheeks like a couple of glass
knobs, and his red hair, whose decisive, precip-
itate ending all around his head left a queer impression that rats, or some larger and more fero-
cious animal, had been his barber. I forget now
whether it was in sport or earnest that I used to
say to myself, that boy's hair had been "chawed
off."

It must have been that his facial aspect, height-
ened, of course, by his winged straw hat, aided
him materially in the expression of his fears with
regard to my safety ; for this cherubic Agamem-
non carried every point in that council of war ;
and it was unanimously resolved that I should
change my quarters.

Accordingly, the next night, I was entertained
in the stable of another of my school-fellows,

residing at the remotest corner of the district. Now I do not want to be considered fastidious or luxurious in my tastes; but I must own to a very loud complaint, entered the morning afterward, against the comparative discomforts of this new lodging. There was very little hay in the stable to which I had been transferred; and the boards, moreover, were very hard indeed. It may have been an improper spirit in which I made the remark; but I went back again to the first school-fellow who has figured in this narrative, and told him if a boy had n't a respectable barn to invite a friend to, he need n't think *I* was going to be his guest, — that 's all!

After watching, for a moment, the impression of my words upon my friend, I said furthermore, that I was going to strike out for myself, as I was growing tired of the monotony of hay-mows and bread-and-butter, anyways. I wanted a change.

Then came one of the most impressive moments that I shall have to chronicle in these memoirs; for, as soon as I had finished speaking, my friend slapped me vigorously on the back, making at the same time, with excited shrillness,

this observation, " Hey ! " — which, being a common juvenile exclamation, had, of course, no
jocose allusion to the principal subject of my
discourse.

" Hey ! bully for you ! " continued my enthusiastic friend and school-fellow, as soon as he
could get his breath, which the suddenness of
his lucky thought had evidently taken away.
" Hey ! that 's just what *I*'d do. I 'd go out into
the world, and seek my fortune, like the boys in
the story-books ; and," said he, suddenly changing his tone and manner to those of the most
excessive gravity and deliberation, — "and, that
you need n't be without means to help you along,
take these ! "

Whereupon he drew forth from his capacious
trousers pocket, and placed in my hand, five
large copper cents, which at first had the appearance of so many oysters fried in batter, so girt
about and covered were they with fragments of
bread-and-butter, deposited, I suppose, in the
course of my friend's entire catering.

It was, indeed, as he assured me, his whole
cash capital ; but he would not hear to my
scruples at taking it. More earnest or impres-

sive about it, or, under the circumstances, more self-denying and truly generous, he could not have been if he had been giving the world away.

So, that morning, we parted, — he wending his way, by no means *con amore*, to school ; and I, with a queer, uncertain feeling in the region of my small waistcoat, going forth, my five coppers in my pocket, to seek my fortune.

CHAPTER IV.

DESERTING entirely the haunts of my play-fellows, I stole down to the wharves. Here the sight of the crowded shipping brought back, more strongly than ever, the memory of that exhilarating trip on the old Indiana, with her sublime brass-band and warlike sheet-iron Indian ; and I tried to " hire out " on a steamboat.

The people to whom I made application eyed me suspiciously, for I was very small of my age. They also asked me a great many disagreeable questions, and generally ended by advising me to go home to my friends, if I had any. My size was manifestly against me. Vainly I assured them I was eleven years old, and my own master. They shook their heads, and told me brusquely to " go ashore."

At last I went on board of a steamer called the Diamond, and, after a little inquiry, found

the steward, — a man with a face like the old
steamer itself, with just seams enough in it, from
long battling with the lake breezes, to give hints
of sturdy timbers, or, I should say, of hidden
strength. His determined mouth ran across his
face like one of the bolted arches across the hur-
ricane-deck, — large, strong, firm. His hair may
be thin and gray now, and his back bent with the
years, — if they have not beached him as they
have the old steamer, and carried him away altogether ; but so great was the impression this man
made on me then, that I think I should still recognize him whenever or wherever we might
chance to meet.

Having, I remember, gone through the usual
colloquy with him as a steward, I assured him as
a man, that I did not know where to go if I did
go ashore, that I had no home and no friends,
and, in a word, so played upon his good nature
that he told me to go into the pantry and go to
work. I obeyed ; that is, I went into the pantry,
and went to work — upon the heartiest meal that
I had ever partaken of up to that date.

The steward meant that I should help a greasy-
looking fellow, whom I found washing dishes

there when I entered. Overcome, however, by the savory smell of meats and other remains of dinner, which had not yet gone down again to the kitchen, the first words I said to the succulent pantryman were framed into a demand for something to eat.

As soon as he recovered his equanimity and his dish-cloth, which latter he had dropped in sheer surprise at what he evidently considered my stupendous impudence, the pantryman wanted to know, bluntly, what I was doing there ; the while he gave his foot such a preliminary flourish as plainly indicated his intention to accelerate my motion thence. I informed him, in considerable haste, that I came by the steward's order. This straightway altered the case in the opinion of the obsequious menial. He now pointed at a row of chafing-dishes, and said, "There it is ; pitch in !"

A few moments afterward the steward found me so absorbed in my "work" that I did not notice his entrance into the pantry. Bread-and-butter in small quantities, and at irregular intervals, had been, it must be owned, rather poor satisfaction to the appetite of a growing boy. The steward must have watched me some time in silence; for my eyes, happening to float away at random in an ecstasy of pleased and vigorous mastication, encountered him, standing not far from my side gazing at me earnestly. I dropped my knife and fork in fear, as he had talked to me like a rough, surly fellow. His voice was wholly changed now, when he spoke; and I noticed it. "Why," he asked, "did n't you tell me you was hungry?"

My only answer was to let my eyes fall from his face to the roast beef and potatoes yet undevoured before me.

"There, eat as much as you want," said the steward, in a softer voice still. "Come to think," he added, "you need n't wash dishes: I 'll use you in the cabin."

For some reason, I had gained a friend in that gruff fellow. Three days later he knocked that same greasy pantryman down for abusing me. Indeed, he fought for me many times afterward as I would gladly fight for him now if I knew where to find him, and if I were sure of the success which always attended him as my champion.

On this craft I must have been working for general results, or for the amateur delight of forming one of a steamboat's crew. I do not remember that anything was ever said about wages, either by myself or the steward. If, in fact, I were called upon to-morrow to make out such a bill for my services as should claim conscientiously just what I earned, I think I should be very much embarrassed; and it would, too, I fancy be a fine piece of mental balancing to decide whether the amateur delight alluded to above was at all equal to the utter sea-sick misery I was called upon to endure.

My duties in the cabin were bounded only by my capacity. I had to help set the table, wait on it, and clear it away; sweep, dust, and make myself generally useful. I did well enough, I suppose, so long as we were in port; but out on the lake, if the waves were at all turbulent, I was much worse than useless. It took me longer to get my sea-legs on than almost any one I have ever known. Some allowance was made for me the first trip; I was permitted, that is, to be as miserable as I could be, and take to my berth as often as I liked.

In the course of time — and it seemed a very
long time — we arrived at Cleveland, where part
of our freight and passengers were landed. No
sooner had the steamer touched the wharf than I
sprang ashore, as the best means of curing my
nausea. By the time I had reached what I take
now to have been Superior Street, I was congratulating myself on my sudden restoration to a better understanding with my rebellious stomach ;
and for the next hour I was at liberty, in the language of an admired poet of our day, to "lean and
loaf at my ease," flattening my nose against shop-
windows.

In connection with my sanitary stroll through
the pretty city of Cleveland, I may mention a
phenomenon — both physical and metaphysical —
which occurred to me, with some of the surprise,
if not the delight, of a discovery. And I look upon it still as a striking instance of the power, not
only of association, but of the mind over the body.
Happening, in a short, narrow street, on my return toward the wharves, to pass a sort of junk-
shop and second-hand clothing-store combined,
my nose became cognizant of a stale, tarry, water-
logged smell, at the same moment that my eyes

lighted upon a sailor hat, shirt, and pantaloons
dangling from a hoop at the door; and — be it believed or not — I am telling the truth, when I say
that I became instantly as sea-sick as ever!

Whether the relapse came from the kelpy scent
of the shop and neighborhood, or from the sight
of the suit of clothes relict of the mariner, or
from the mental and stomachic association of
both with scenes I had just passed through on
the lake, I cannot of course, at this distance of
time, presume to determine. I recollect, however, I had a droll, boyish impression, for a long
while afterward, in connection with those second-
hand, sail-cloth trousers. There was, indeed, as
I recall them even now, something strangely suggestive of hopeless infirmity about them. As
they flapped and bulged wearily in the tar-laden
zephyrs, the knees would become full and, in some
inexplicable way, would give ghostly hints of the
knock-kneed idiosyncrasies of the late wearer.
Then the whole garment would become mysteriously distended, as if some poor mariner were
being hanged by the neck, and the choking and
plethora had reached even to the very ends of
his pantaloons; reminding me quite vividly, the

while, of a pair of piratical legs — which a sailor in the forecastle of our steamer, the Diamond, had shown me in the frontispiece of a very greasy book — dangling pictorially from the gibbet of the lamented Captain Kidd.

Well, what I set out to say is, that for a long time afterward I held the juvenile opinion that those same second-hand sailor trousers, big at the bottom, and little at the top, like the churn in the venerable riddle, were alone what made me then so suddenly and so mysteriously sea-sick. I did not, however, think much about it at the time, or of anything else, but getting back with all possible expedition to the steamer and to bed.

Sea-sickness, you may have observed, is very much like first love. While it lasts, you rarely get any sympathy from those not affected like yourself; and when it is over, you are the first to laugh at it. And there is always likely to be something ludicrous about it — in the memory; but, *durante bello*, it is serious enough, in all conscience. Now the second voyage of our steamer Diamond was a remarkably calm one; and I, true to the instincts of your convalescent, whether of nausea or erotomania, ridiculed my previous troubles. But on the third voyage the lake was rougher than ever. I fought my weakness valiantly ; yet it seemed a battle against all visible Nature, — the water, the sky, and the crazy old steamboat, to say nothing of my own recalcitrant little body. I was forced to yield.

I had, however, been a sailor too long for any faint show of sympathy. The steward, too, was short of help ; and there was no escape for me. I was accordingly called out to do duty at the dinner-table, where I staggered about under plates and platters to the terror of all immediate beholders. I had little or no control of my legs and hands ; and my head, if I remember correctly now, was engaged in framing and passing silent resolutions of want of confidence in my stomach.

Having emptied a dish of stewed chicken into the lap of an uncomplaining lady-passenger, who was nearly as sick as I was, but who was ashamed to own it, I planted my back violently against the side of the cabin, in the inane endeavor to steady the rolling ship or my rolling head, — I did not know or care exactly which. While thus employed, I heard the grating voice of the captain, who was, if possible, always as ill-natured as he looked.

"Here, boy!" he called.

I went to him, staggering and trembling, and apprehending all manner of vengeance.

"What are you staring at, you lubber? Why don't you turn me a glass of water?"

From which comparatively amiable speech of my commander, I was left in doubt whether he was aware of my late exploit with the stewed chicken. I seized an unwieldy water-pitcher; and, just as I had it well elevated, the boat gave a perverse lunge, and I proceeded, dizzier than ever, to pour the entire contents of the jug into the captain's ear, and down his neck. Everything for a yard or so around, excepting only his goblet, received some share of the water.

I did not tarry long to observe the rage of the captain; but what I did see, and more especially hear of it, was certainly as intense and loud and blasphemous as anything of the kind that has since come within the range of my perception. The pitcher broke on the floor where I dropped it; and I fled back to my berth, and covered up my head.

My commander did not pursue me ; but about an hour afterward the steward came to me with a very long face, as I observed with the one eye which I uncovered long enough to ask him if the captain had seen me deposit the stewed chicken in the lap of that lady.   No : I was told the captain had not heard of that, but was sufficiently wroth about the wetting he had received at my hands ; and the steward ended by saying that I would have to go ashore at the next landing.   He was very sorry, he assured me ; but the captain was inexorable.

I hastened to inform my friend and protector that I would be glad to set my foot on any dry land whatsoever, and that I never wanted to go on a steamboat any more ; for the vessel, now in the trough of the sea, was rolling and creaking more violently every minute, and my nausea had increased in proportion.

The next landing, the steward gave me to understand, was Conneaut, Ohio, which was his own home.   He comforted me, furthermore, with the assurance that his wife would be down at the wharf to get the linen, which she washed for the steamer ; and that she should take me home with her.

The pier of Conneaut, where we finally arrived, was now invested with absorbing interest to me. I wondered which of the tanned faces that looked up from the dock belonged to my future mistress ; and I wondered, too, which of the weather-beaten fishermen's huts along the shore — about the only habitations in sight — was to be my future home. I hoped it was the one with the little boats before it on the beach, and the long fish-nets spread out to dry ; where the white gulls seemed to make their head-quarters, wheeling about the little roof, or sliding up against the sky, or swooping the surf, and skimming along the billows of the lake.

I was thus musing, in grateful convalescence, on the upper-deck, when the steward approached, and pointed me out to his wife. She was, as I remember her, a chubby, black-eyed little person, with a pleasant voice. At her woman's question as to whether I had my things all packed and ready, I became embarrassed ; but the steward helped me out by answering for me, " Yes, he has 'em on his back."

The knowledge of my forlorn condition, and a sudden choking sensation in the throat, came upon the good little woman at one and the same time, as I was made aware by an attempt to speak, which she abandoned, substituting — very much to the lowering of my boyish pride — a fear-less and vigorous hugging, together with a hearty, loud-sounding kiss, right before the passengers, the greasy pantryman, and others of the crew.

Then the steward's wife, without another word, hurried me ashore into a one-horse wagon, with the soiled linen, and drove away up to the village, which was a mile or two from the lake.

CHAPTER V.

NEAR the end of a quiet street we alighted at a little frame-house, all embowered in peach and plum trees. This was the steward's home, and soon was as much mine as if I held the title-deed. They had no children, and the steward's wife was not long in growing wonderfully fond of me, — so fond, indeed, that she humored me in everything.

When tired of the house and little yard, I amused myself in strolling alone to the lake and taking amateur voyages in the fishermen's boats, without their permission ; and in swimming and fishing and hunting clams in Conneaut Creek, or River, whichever it is called. My favorite bathing-place was beneath the high bridge which the curious reader can cross any day on the Lake Shore Railroad.

When the steamer arrived, the steward's wife

and I went down to the pier, in the one-horse wagon, with the clean clothes of the last washing, and brought away the money for it, together with a new load of soiled linen.

This one-horse equipage, by the way, must have belonged to some neighbor, for I do not remember that we ever brought it into requisition, except for laundry purposes. Nor do I remember that I ever imperilled my neck, or the horse's, with it alone, as would surely have been the case if it had been our property.

Our practice was, invariably, to spend the money for the last washing before the next one was begun ; and this was the routine to which we scrupulously adhered :

The steward's wife, namely, would use the first day after the steamer had gone in baking all manner of bread, pies, and cakes ; enough, in fact, to last us until the good ship Diamond should come round again. Then, on the second day, we would go to the village livery-stable, and get a horse and buggy, with which we would ride five miles out in the country, and "visit" at the farm-house of her father and mother. Having thus exhausted all her earnings, we would return home on the third day, and the steward's wife would go very contentedly about her washing.

This may not have been the best sort of economy for a poor washerwoman, but it was certainly a most delightful way for a thoughtless boy to pass his time. Counting out an occasional tendency to biliousness consequent upon over-doses of the good things of her regular first-day's baking, I must say, the weeks I spent with that good, simple-hearted creature were very happy ones indeed.

Her kindness extended even to the tattered places of my scanty wardrobe. Everything was made whole and clean. She bought me, I remember, a shirt for fifty cents, and made over a pair of her husband's summer pantaloons to fit me ; so that I was not, as formerly, confined to the house while my solitary piece of linen was in laundry.

There was only one grievous alloy, thereafter, in my complete happiness, and that was in the shape of some much larger boys than myself, who diverted their minds by whipping me whenever and wherever they could lay hands on me. I

fought them at first, but I always came off beaten;
and so I gave it up, and it is due to the nimble-
ness of my legs, or to the exceeding elasticity
inherent in terror, to add that they rarely or
never caught me after that.   Still the grievance
was all the same.

On one occasion, however, the steward stopped
over at home a trip, and, being informed of the
persecutions to which I had been subjected, he
gave a sound drubbing to every one of my enemies,
and threatened them with the repetition of the
same as often as I should complain.   I had the
satisfaction of witnessing this castigation, which,
though somewhat informal, — being administered
when each of my foes was "down," as I may say,
across my champion's knee, in a species of
"chancery" not yet introduced, I believe, into the
prize ring, — had, nevertheless, the desired effect.
The peace was preserved, and I was happy.

But perfect happiness is short-lived, after all.
It was not many weeks later when we were
startled in our little home by a call in the interest
of my relatives, conveying the intelligence that
my whereabout was known, and that I should be
sent for soon.

Now it happened that the steamer Diamond
was due at the pier the afternoon succeeding
the one on which we had heard this appalling
piece of news. I said nothing to my benefac-
tress of my design, formed almost instantane-
ously ; for I knew she would not consent to its
carrying out. But, when the steamer had left,
I was not to be found in any of the fishermen's
boats on the lake, or throwing stones at the gulls
along the shore, or afterward beneath the high
bridge, or in any of my usual haunts in the
village.

I had, in fact, stowed myself away in the
old Diamond's forecastle, where I was not discovered till Conneaut was well out of sight. Unfortunately, my new shirt and pantaloons were
both in the wash at the time; and I have never
seen them since. Thus I came away with the
same well-worn clothes and solitary piece of linen
in which I had first fled from Buffalo. The five
coppers I still had in my pocket, kept, I know
not by what queer inspiration, against future
needs.

I never heard from her lips how much the

steward's wife grieved at my sudden disappear-
ance, for I never saw the good soul afterward ;
but, from what I have since learned, I scarcely
hope ever again, by anything that I may do, or
that may happen to me, to produce such a void
in the heart of any living being. I had taken
the place, I suppose, in her childless bosom, of
that strongest and purest of all affections, — the
mother's for her offspring.

Several years afterward she "nearly killed
with kindness" a friend of mine — to use the
language of the friend herself — who gave her
news from me. I should hardly mention this
now, were it not for the sequel, which further
illustrates, I think, though in a sad way, the
real goodness and constancy of the poor creature's heart, while going to show at the same
time what a warm place was won in it by a
graceless vagabond.

Later in her life some great sorrow — the
exact nature of which I never learned — un-
hinged her intellect ; and her insanity took the
mild form of always expecting me back, the
same homeless urchin, unchanged by the years.
It was, as I have intimated, in the afternoon

when I left her; and, until she was moved from that part of the country to an asylum where she was cared for in comfort till she died, she used to go regularly every afternoon to the friend above mentioned and ask about her " lost boy," as she called me.

CHAPTER VI.

THE CONTUMELY OF CAPTAINS.

THE captain of the steamer Diamond, never in the habit of looking pleased at anything, did not depart from his habit, but rather carried it to an unwonted degree of frowning and darkling excess, when he saw me at work again about the table, at the next meal after leaving Conneaut. He said nothing to me, however, but, calling up the steward, had a long, stormy talk with him.

The steward in self-defence was, of course, obliged to tell how I had stowed myself away in the forecastle, which, I need not say, did not enhance the commander's opinion of me. What that irate gentleman would have done with me — whether he would not have thrown me bodily into the lake if it had not been for the earnest deprecation of the steward — is even yet, in quiet, reflective moments, an interesting problem to my mind.

At last the captain's unwilling consent was obtained to take me back to Buffalo, where, as my intercessor said, I had friends. It happened that the steamer was bound up the lake to Toledo, where, also, I had relatives, — a fact which I did not make known to the steward. I was now compassed about, it will be seen, by prospects of capture on every hand. I had my reasons, nevertheless, for wishing to be left at Buffalo instead of Toledo. The latter city was so small that my relatives would easily lay hold of me there ; and the former, being not only a larger city, but so much farther away, I should stand a much better chance of concealment, and, what was of almost equal importance, I should be sure of an additional week's board before the steamer reached there.

At Toledo, therefore, I scarcely went ashore at all. During the return trip to Buffalo my mind was exceeding busy with daring and mighty schemes of escape from the steward, whom circumstances had now metamorphosed into a walking terror to me. That honest fellow had confided to me that he considered it his duty, and for my interests, to have an interview with the people

from whom I had fled, and to do I know not what
other appalling things toward providing me with
a suitable, permanent home.

I did not, however, think it prudent to express
my demurrer at his prospective proceedings,
choosing secretly to trust the hope of sustaining
it rather to my legs than to my eloquence. Accordingly, when we had arrived at Buffalo, I
watched my opportunities, and, seizing the right
moment, fled precipitately up the docks, unob-
served by my well-meaning, self-imposed guardian.

Two hours subsequently, deeming myself safe,
I walked boldly on board of the old steamer Baltic.
Here, by a wonderful freak of fortune, it was not
ten minutes till I had "shipped" as cabin-boy, at
the marvellous salary of ten dollars a month.
Surely, I have never felt so rich or independent
since. I went to work with a will, inspired to
undertake anything, in any weather, by a calm
sense of security, and by the princely guerdon
which loomed high in my imagination at the
end of the month. In the course of time, too,
I am happy to say here incidentally, I over-

came completely my remarkable tendency to sea-sickness.

The Baltic, then having seen her best days, did not belong to any regular line, but went roll-ing and creaking about on roaming commissions for freight and passengers all over the lakes. Up to the time of the inglorious *dénouement* in which my life as one of her crew ended, I can remember nothing of moment which happened, except that the sense of my own importance and of my accumulating wealth grew daily in strict proportion ; and that her captain was a perpet-ual mountain to me, bearing down very hard on my expansive spirit, but never quite crushing it.

With a few exceptions, indeed, my experiences with captains were strikingly disagreeable, but not, I think, peculiar. From actual brutality, or a mistaken sense of duty, — applying especially to boys and common sailors, — your ordinary cap-tain, on lake or ocean, has often seemed to me, in some respects, less human than the ship over which he tyrannizes. With regard to this cold autocrat of the venerable steamer Baltic I rec-ollect a queer, boyish fancy I entertained, I for-get whether in earnest or in sportive retribution ;

3 *

namely, that the Nor'westers had not only piled up the breakers which threatened continually in the hard, wrinkled folds and lines of his face, but had also blown the warmth, and, in a word, all the heart out of his voice and manner.

As the month drew near its close, however, and the ten dollars earned by my own hands were soon to be mine, the contumely of my commander had little weight against the buoyancy and growing independence of my spirit. I had been in the Baltic just three weeks and four days on the eventful morning when she was to leave Toledo. It had been my habit, once a week, to wash my only shirt in the pantry and to wait about the kitchen till it dried, with my coat buttoned up to my chin. Now, on this same morning, I had just issued from the latter place with my clean shirt in my hand, when the captain told me to do something, — I forget what. I assured him I would as soon as I could put on my shirt. He told me to do it right away, at the same time coupling me and my garment blasphemously together, and consigning us, figuratively, to a port where, for aught I know, there may be many collectors but no custom-houses.

I gave the captain to understand, still more bluntly, that I would do nothing till I had made my toilet ; and, inspired by a memory of former wrongs, as well as a consciousness of prospective opulence, I used to my superior officer other language of a saucy and independent kind. Whereupon the captain, in sailor phrase, "tacked" for me, and I "tacked" for the shore. Here, then, I demanded my pay ; but the enraged commander solemnly averred that he would see me first in that tropical port just alluded to, and *then* I should never have a cent.

Shortly after, the boat pushed off into the stream. A sympathizing friend threw me a paper of crackers from the pantry on the upper deck ; and, as the Baltic got under way, there I stood on the wharf, with my paper of crackers in one hand, and my only shirt in the other, clamoring for my wages.

I stood leaning against the splintered pile, which had been one of her hitching-posts, and watched the Baltic as she faded slowly out of sight. My courage seemed to fade with her. It was not the loss of my place and probably of my dinner that crushed me, but — after so many wealthy dreams — this utter financial ruin! What were my five coppers, still jingling loosely in my pocket, to the dollars I had lost, or to the combined capital of my relatives in that very city? The contest was plainly hopeless. For as much as a half-hour I considered myself delivered bound into the hands of my pursuers. Indeed, the dock on which I was making this mental soliloquy happened to be but a short distance from the warehouse of an uncle of mine, then a commission-merchant and ship-owner in Toledo.

At last, I betook myself despondently to a neighboring shed and donned my shirt, and then, as under some desperate spell, walked straight toward my uncle's office. I crossed the threshold and saw him in conversation with some gentlemen. While waiting till he should notice me, I beheld, through the office window, the little steamer Arrow, almost ready to start for Detroit. I knew that the Baltic was also going to Detroit, and thought that I might possibly get my money if I followed her thither. Only those unfortunate persons who have been suddenly prevented from committing suicide when in the very act will thoroughly understand, I think, the feeling with which I hailed this thought. Instantly my comprehensive vow to have nothing more to do with relatives flashed across my mind.

Seeing that my uncle had not yet observed me, I turned quickly on my heel, and made hastily for the dock of the steamer Arrow. I concealed myself on board of her till she was under way, when, making my case known to the steward, I was allowed to work my passage in the cabin to Detroit.

It was that season when, as many dwellers by the Western lakes will remember, the Arrow was the fastest boat on those waters. We passed the other steamer somewhere off Monroe lighthouse ; and on the same afternoon, therefore, as the old Baltic came up to the wharf at Detroit, there I stood before the astonished eyes of her captain, again clamoring for my wages, — with this difference only, that my shirt was now on my back, and my crackers carefully stowed away in my pocket with my five coppers.

CHAPTER VII.

ALMOST A TRAGEDY.

AS soon as the Baltic was made fast, and the captain had sufficiently recovered from his astonishment, he stalked toward me, denouncing vengeance. I took to my heels as soon as he reached the wharf. Finding that he could not catch me, he stopped, shook his fist, and swore he would arrest me if he saw or heard anything more of me. I, of course, knew nothing of the law but its terrors, and, though I really had the better side in the case, gave the matter up.

It may have been that the joy to be in a strange city, out of the way of capture, helped me materially, but it seems a little remarkable now how soon this mighty disappointment and defeat vanished wholly from my thoughts. I cannot remember that the circumstance ever crossed my mind again till I was called upon, months subsequently, to recount my adventures to admiring school-fellows.

It could not, I am sure, have been twenty
minutes after my Parthian contest with the irate
captain — for, if the truth must be told, I shot
him a scathing epithet or so in my flight —
when I was amusing myself after the manner of
the "light and heavy balancer," rolling myself
about upon the tops of some white-fish barrels,
at a neighboring dock, as contented and happy
as a thoughtless boy only can be.

Tied to this dock was a little sloop-rigged
scow, used in bringing sand from Hog Isl-
and in the Detroit River. There was a small
boat, with a solitary oar and scull-hole belonging to this sand-scow, tugging lazily at the rope
by which it was attached, as it floated dreamily
astern in the current. A youngish fellow, with
a good-natured face, was engaged in unloading
the larger craft when I espied the smaller one.

Now, if there was any one thing in which much
practice and a boundless love had lent me any
degree of skill, it was risking my life in amateur
navigation. I need scarcely tell you, therefore,
how I ceased my acrobatics with the white-fish
barrels, and came and gazed wistfully at that little boat ; how I varied this employment by star-

ing inquiringly into the mild face of that enviable
young man who had control of its destinies ; how,
when he paused in his work to regard me in turn,
I thrust my hands unconcernedly into my pockets, and looked studiously away from him and the
little boat, at the far windings of the broad river ;
how, when he had resumed his work, my eyes also
resumed their longing pilgrimage from the little
boat to his face ; and how, having repeated this
process several times, my mind tugging fitfully
and dreamily at its purpose, as the little boat at
its rope, I finally turned and asked, in an abrupt
voice, for the loan of the one-oared craft.

The young man was startled into a smile, perhaps of sheer good-nature, and perhaps of pleased
surprise at so brief a petition overtoppled by so
lengthy an enacted preamble. Certainly, he said,
I might take his little boat, and I embarked.

Pushing boldly into the stream, which runs
there three or four miles an hour, I sculled vigorously for the Canadian shore. Even at this early
period, I may remark, I had an overpowering desire to visit foreign lands ; and I resolved to take
that opportune occasion to go abroad. Those
most familiar with the swift, deep river will best

understand that the probability of my reaching the British shore was only less than the possibility of my ever getting back again ; and that the project, under the circumstances, was utterly mad and perilous.

I sculled out well toward the middle of the stream, exulting, boy-like, in the wild freedom of the voyage ; heading diagonally against the current, but, otherwise, taking very little heed whither the prow of my boat was pointing. Suddenly I noticed a commotion on the shore I had left, and looked curiously among the people there for the cause. Every one seemed now pointing and hallooing at me. It must be, I concluded, they were applauding my skill and daring ; and, thus encouraged, I sculled more lustily than ever, with my back still toward the bow of my boat.

Not many moments afterward I heard, rising above the other noises of the busy life around and on the river, a queer, rumbling sound in the water ahead of me. I turned to find a large steamboat making directly toward me, under full speed, and not more than two or three rods away. I dropped my oar and stood paralyzed with the

E

sudden danger and the utter hopelessness of escape.

The people on the steamer seemed nearly as terrified as myself, for they shouted and waved their hands and arms in the wildest manner. The bow of the large vessel just grazed that of my little one when the great paddle-wheels were stopped. The swell caused by the motion of the steamer struck the small craft and threw it clear of the wheel ; and the Niagara, for that was her name, passed by on her voyage.

If the wheel had been stopped twenty seconds later, my boat and myself would most certainly have been drawn into it, and circumstances over which I could have had no control would, in all probability, have prevented me from writing out this faithful account of my adventures.

I now put my boat about and sculled for shore, abandoning my scheme of foreign travel and exploration. The long and difficult struggle with the current which ensued should have been enough, without the terrible fright I had experienced, to bring me, I think, to a realizing sense of the wildness and madness of my undertaking. Finally reaching the dock and making the yawl

fast to the sand-scow, I exchanged a very sheepish sort of smile for the good-humored or sympathetic one of the young man, her captain, and
strolled off leisurely over the wharf, out of the
way of the curious people who had been the witnesses of my exploit.

In a remarkably short time thereafter I was
engaged again in rolling myself about on the top
of the white-fish barrels ; thinking no more of my
hairbreadth escape, or of what was to become of
me in the immediate future. Twenty minutes, as
nearly as I can recollect, were about as long as
any direst misfortune, at that period, could cloud
the brightness of my young hope. This utter
recklessness I can scarcely understand now. It
requires, I suppose, more years and experience
than I had then to learn the knack of despairing.

At least, I know I was in the full delight of
my first freedom, and, in all these boyish wanderings, the fact that I was in need of a meal
or a night's lodging would occur to me, almost
always, as a sudden inspiration, and only at the
usual hour for the meal or for going to bed.
The joy of my solitary, Robinson-Crusoe life, on

the wharves and among the white-fish barrels, was so strong upon me that I suffered much less than would at first be imagined from the hunger which sometimes filled the long intervals between one meal and the next.

I have just used the words " solitary life," and I have used them advisedly ; for I can remember only one juvenile friend whom I ever picked up as a companion in my vagrancy, and that was an urchin of Irish descent.   We met on the wharf, at Detroit, if my memory does not fail me, some days after the events just chronicled.   He was the first and last whom I took into my boyish confidence, for the companionship was not harmonious, and ended in the disaster of a bloody nose, which he inflicted on me at parting.   This, with the black eye which I bestowed in turn upon him, was, I believe, the only ceremony observed on the occasion of our mutual leave-taking.

Toward evening of the day of my narrow escape in the yawl of the sand-scow, I drew from my pocket the crackers thrown to me that morning, at Toledo, from the pantry of the Baltic, and seated myself on the wharf overlooking the clear

river to eat them, feeding the minnows with the
crumbs. When it began to be dark, it suddenly
occurred to me that I had no place to sleep. I am
sure that up to that moment the subject of my
prospective lodgings had not crossed my mind.
I arose, and, brushing the last fragments of my
crackers down to my fellow-vagabonds, the minnows, I walked toward the place where the sand-
scow was moored.

I remembered now the good-natured face of
the young fellow who had so willingly loaned me
his small boat and never scolded me for the peril
to which I had exposed it, as well as myself.
Arrived in the little cabin of the scow, I found
him already retired. I had conscientious scruples
about begging, and imagined I was doing nothing
of the kind when I made the simple affirmative
statement of my case. Indeed, I would not have
had time to append any request to my first sentence, for the young man, in his prompt kindness,
told me, as soon as he had heard I had no lodging
of my own, that I was welcome to share his,
making for me, while he spoke, a place on the
loose hay which formed his bed.

A solitary pillow-case of coarse sheeting, stuffed

with hay, was the only thing like bedding discoverable.   Here I threw myself without undressing and tried to sleep ; but there were more lodgers with us, bred, I suppose, by the sand, than even the good-hearted fellow would have willingly accommodated, — that is, if he felt them as I did. Before morning, however, youth and fatigue got the better of them, and I slept soundly.

CHAPTER VIII.

ARISING refreshed, I sallied forth early on the wharf to amuse myself. In the course of an hour it occurred to me suddenly — out of no more previous thought or care about the matter than I had had the night before on the subject of a lodging — that I had had no breakfast, and could not say exactly where I was going to get any.

The good-natured face of my late bedfellow again suggested itself to my mind, and I returned to the sand-scow. There he was in the little coop of a cabin, just partaking of his morning meal, which consisted of a small baker's loaf and a tea-cup of molasses. Still humoring my scruples as to direct begging, I gave him to understand, affirmatively, that I did not know where to get my breakfast.

Without uttering a word, the good fellow broke

his loaf in two and gave me half. In fact, I cannot recollect that he ever asked me any questions ; if he did, they were of such a kindly nature as not in any way to suggest the ignominious close of my free career by capture, and that is why, I suppose, I have forgotten them. We dipped our bread by turns into the teacup of molasses very amicably, and took alternate draughts of the pure river water from the same tin dipper.

Even now as I write I can see again the strange light in his honest eyes, just behind the surprise with which they regarded me, when, our simple meal over, I drew slowly from my pocket my five copper cents, and placed them in his hand. Of course, he would not take them. It was, no doubt, because they were my entire wealth that I straightway received the impression that he thought them too much for his somewhat meagre hotel accommodations, and so I recalled to his memory that he had also loaned me his small boat the afternoon before.

"Never mind, never mind," he said ; "put your money away. You can take the small boat again if you want to."

These were his exact words ; and there was

more true feeling in the way he said them than would go to make up many a longer speech I have since heard, in the pathos of melodrama, where the hero has magnanimously refused vast estates and lacs of rupees. (If the reader will excuse the parenthesis, I should like to be allowed to say, right here, God bless that young fellow — or middle-aged fellow now — wherever he is!)

Whether a sudden apprehension of future and direr exigencies, or a gleam of my usual delight in small boats, or both together, flashed across my mind at that moment, I am not now prepared to state ; but I remember I did put my money away, and, climbing down again into the little yawl, amused myself by imperilling my life once more in the swift current. This time, however, I ventured merely on short coasting voyages around the docks. At least, I had not yet come to a decision about the feasibility of taking in something foreign in my way, being in the very act of casting a pair of longing eyes at the Canadian shore, when I was hailed by my friend of the sand-scow, and requested to bring the boat to land.

A favorable breeze had sprung up, and the

4

scow, now discharged of her sand, took her departure for a new load. I stood on the wharf and
waved her adieu ; and that was the last I ever
saw of her, or of the noble fellow who united in
his own person her captain, mates, and crew.

I may have felt a little more alone in the world
now, for I remember I did not go back to my
jolly play-fellows, the white-fish barrels, but
boarded divers steamboats instead, in quest of
work. I received the same prompt answer from
all. They did not want me. As will be supposed,
my one suit of clothes was by this time beginning
to show marks of the service it had done among
the greasy platters of pantries and cabins. This
fact, probably, was the greatest barrier to my success, and the cause, too, of most of the rough language I received in answer to my applications.

Toward night I became desperately hungry,
for, it will be remembered, my last warm meal was
the dinner of the day before eaten upon the little
steamer Arrow, on the way from Toledo. Weary
with repeated refusals from steward after steward,
I went boldly at last on board of the steamer
Pacific and inquired for the captain.

It was straightway demanded of me what such a beggar as I wanted of the captain. I resented the term "beggar" immediately: I purposed to work for what I got ; I had money, if it came to that, in proof of which I jingled defiantly the five pennies in my pocket. No ; I was no beggar, but I must see the captain.

Carrying my point, finally, I was led to the room of the commander, whom I found to be a short, red-faced man with a voice like a nor'-wester. He was leaning back on a camp-chair, with his feet in a berth, and smoking his after-supper cigar. To his gruff "What do you want with *me?*" I replied meekly that I desired to wash dishes or do anything for something to eat, that I had had nothing but a few crackers and some bread and molasses in thirty-six hours, that I had applied to his steward that afternoon and had been refused, and that I was forced finally to come to him hungry and wanting work.

"What's your name?" demanded the captain ; "and who are you, and where do you come from ?"

I answered the first part of his question, but he noticed I hesitated after that. He gave me

laconically to understand that I must tell him
who I was, or starve for all of him.   I was forced
to comply ; that is, saying nothing about Buffalo,
I mentioned my uncle, the ship-owner in Toledo.

This was a fatal mistake, as I learned very
soon to my sorrow.   The captain's eye became suddenly and maliciously bright, and his face redder
than ever.   For as many as ten awful seconds he
mangled his cigar fiercely and silently between
his teeth.   Then there proceeded from his
mouth, in addition to the smoke he had swallowed in his wrath, a terrible volley of oaths and
curses, of which my uncle's heart and eyes were
the objects.

This captain, as came to my knowledge afterward, had been discharged from the employ of
my uncle for some shortcoming or other ; and
he now proposed, it seems, to take his revenge.
He sent hastily for one of the cabin-waiters, and
ordered him, in my hearing, to take me to a state-
room, give me a light supper, and then lock me
in.

" I 'm goin'," said the captain, — and how well I
remember his words, — " I 'm goin' to take him to

the House of Vagrancy in the mornin' ; and then
write to that old villain, his uncle, to come and
take him out." The captain furthermore told the
waiter to "bear a hand" and keep me safe,
till he should call for me the next morning. He
always thought, and now he was sure, he would
get even with that uncle of mine, whose pride he
was going to take down ; and I was borne away
through another deluge of the captain's oaths.

Of course the thought was very wrong, com-
prehending as it did many innocent and well-
meaning people, but it seemed to me then, in
that brief moment of despair, that all my troubles
sprang from the fact that I was so unfortunate as
to have wealthy relatives. They were the first
and last cause of all my grief. The earth, I felt
sure, was not broad enough to escape them in.
Among the peach and plum trees of Conneaut,
or in the jungle of the crowded shipping at Detroit, the far-reaching fate was upon me. Though
my small body was disguised in rags, still my own
hunger wrought and spoke in the interests of
those from whom it appeared hopeless to flee.
And, more on their account than mine, I was

now on my way to that place of unknown terror, the House of Vagrancy.

The captain's room was on the main deck, and the state-room to which I was to be conducted was on the deck above. I was so terrified, or so small, that my jailer, the waiter, thought it safe, as well as more convenient, to release his hold of my collar, and allow me to precede him up the stairs.

Now there was another companion-way on the opposite side of the steamer, corresponding to that up which we were to go ; and as soon as we had attained the middle of the upper cabin I sprang out of the reach of my conductor and down the opposite stairs at about three jumps. I fled to the shore and up the docks with all the speed that my deathly terror lent me.

I could hear my pursuer after me, but it was already dark, and I could hardly have seen him if I had dared to look around. I succeeded in reaching one of the vast piles of coal which the good people of Detroit will remember as standing formerly on the wharf of the Michigan Central steamers. Here I concealed myself.

It was probably a half-hour before my jailer gave up the search, but it seemed four hours at least to me then. Twice he passed very near my hiding-place, and, I recollect, I was afraid lest he should hear the noise of my heart-beats ; they sounded so terribly loud in my frightened ears. I heard him, at last, returning to the steamer, as I had reason to think, for lights and people to aid him.

Then I stole away noiselessly up toward the town, keeping a large coal-pile studiously between me and the place where my pursuer had disappeared ; until, turning a corner I took a side-street which led me, as I supposed, into the heart of the city. What, therefore, was my horror when, after walking for about ten minutes, in this and other crooked thoroughfares, I again found myself suddenly on the lower end of the wharf where lay the steamer Pacific and her dreadful captain !

Once more I took to my heels, and this time succeeded in finding a street which led me, without further mishap, into one of the Avenues.

CHAPTER IX.

WANDERING about for what seemed a long while, turning from one thorough-fare into another, so as to make pursuit uncertain, it finally crossed my mind that it was past my bedtime. Fear had driven away my hunger so completely that I thought no more of it till the next day.

Brushing and rubbing as much of the coal-dust from my clothes as I could, I now walked boldly up to the counter of the Commercial Hotel, and said that I wanted to see the head-porter.

The clerk eyed me curiously as he asked me what I desired of the head-porter. I wanted, I said, to black boots for a night's lodging. The clerk called the chief-porter, and they both looked at me as a natural curiosity, I suppose, while they plied me with a few questions. They seemed

pleased with my answers, or touched by my forlorn condition or my extreme youth, and decided
that I might have a night's lodging without blacking boots for it.

Accordingly one of my questioners conducted
me up into the highest story of the building, and,
pointing to a bed in a large dormitory, left me in
the society of some dozen or more snoring waiters
and cooks. I knew in an instant the nature of
the occupation of my room-mates, for I recognized on entering the apartment that post-culi-
nary smell of dish-water with which custom had
rendered me familiar, and which the philosophic
nostril will, I think, almost always detect about
those whose constant business it is to prepare or
serve the prandial dish.

When I think of that dark dormitory now, and
the sounds that rose from it, I am reminded of a
midsummer night's frog-pond; but I regarded it
far more seriously then. I know not by what
chain of reasoning I established the connection
between their stertorous idiosyncrasies and their
waking employments, yet I remember very dis-
tinctly that I occupied myself, until I fell asleep,
in assigning the proper rank and position to each

of the snorers. The barytone, that came to me through the darkness from the far corner, I concluded, after some deliberation, was that of the chief-cook himself.

Then there was a deep bass, — the real Mephistophelian hero of that opera of sleepers, — whose exact whereabout in the room I could never quite discover, for his note sounded each time in the place farthest from the one where I had heard it last, or expected to hear it next; this *basso cantante,* I had not the slightest doubt, — and I crouched lower on my pillow at the thought, — was that most inscrutable and relentless of tyrants, in all dining-halls and cabins, the head-waiter.

The several tenors, distributed all round me a little too lavishly perhaps for the nicer harmonies of strict musical taste, being — as I suppose, now, in the light of a larger experience — ambitious and fitful, as is the proverbial wont of tenors, and running jealously ever and anon into a dishonest *falsetto,* as if with a professional wish to attract attention, — these several tenor-snorers were, I felt sure, what the world might very well suffer a great many ambitious, fitful, and dishonest tenors always to be, namely, among the common rank and file of cooks and waiters.

And I had firmly made up my mind, long before I was lulled to sleep by the steady *crescendo* of the chorus, that the tapering treble which piped darkling, like some night bird, high over all, proceeded from some pale-faced, meek-eyed scullion of the outer kitchen, who, awake and in the presence of his chief, would not dare say his soul was his own.

I slept soundly enough till about five o'clock the next morning, when I arose hurriedly. Whether my half-roused operatic company of the night before thought me a ghost, or how they explained my mysterious coming and going among them, I did not wait to learn. Leaving them to stare at one another in drowsy amazement, I stole noiselessly and breakfastless away from the hotel.

The fright of the evening preceding had shaken my confidence in human nature generally. I cannot tell how, but I became impressed with the ludicrous idea that the hotel clerk or porter would take my five coppers away from me, in payment for my lodging, — to say nothing of my breakfast, if I should stay for it. So I went down to the docks of the lower part of the city, as far from the Pacific and her captain as possible.

Here I had the good fortune to strike a bargain with the cook of a lumber schooner to wash his dishes for him, provided he should first give me all I could eat; and thus I broke my fast of twenty-four hours with the first full meal I had taken in forty-eight hours.

While finishing up the work I had agreed to do I saw the steamer Pacific passing down the stream, on her voyage away from Detroit, and I breathed freely once more.

I spent some days now, doing odd jobs for cooks and pantrymen for my board and lodging, while their vessels were in port; but my clothes were so worn and soiled by this and previous service that I could get no chance to work for wages as cabin-boy. Because of my clothes, also, no steamer would allow me to go out of port with her; for I was told that there was a law, then existing in most of the lake cities, by which a boat was made responsible for the support of all vagrants she carried into a town.

I do not know whether this was the case; I know merely that I was invariably sent ashore on the departure of any craft for which I had been washing dishes or scouring knives. It was indeed a precarious existence that I led in this way, but one to which I could see no immediate end. I think it was twice I went with but two meals in forty-eight hours, getting nothing from breakfast to breakfast.

And, I may say here, I have always attributed great advantage to the fact that — after the short and disastrous companionship with my young friend of Irish descent, mentioned some pages back — I was my own *fidus Achates* in all these worst distresses.

Two boys will, certainly, do more mischief together than half a dozen will do separately; three boys together will do more than eighteen separately, — and so on. In short, I fancy it may be laid down as a general principle, that, under the conditions just enunciated, there is an increasing geometrical ratio between the number of boys and the amount of evil they will do.

I have alluded before to an account of these

experiences which I gave to my school-fellows months afterward. The degree of fertile suggestion which even the narrative stirred up in my auditory should have made me thankful then, as I am certainly now, that I did thus lead my vagabond life alone. These ardent youngsters would interpolate, in the very thickest and thrillingest movements of my story, advice as to what I should have done, or hints as to what they would have done, under the circumstances.

During this narration to my school-fellows — and now I am coming to the purpose of the present digression — a boy with a very sinister-looking face, who has since happily died of the small-pox, asked me why I did n't *steal,* averring, with great frankness, that was what he would have done.

Now that was the very first time the idea of stealing ever crossed my mind, in connection with my boyish calamities and deprivations. I am sure of this, for I remember the startling impression made upon me at the moment of the boy's suggestion. I dare not say that I would not have stolen, after some of my long fasts, — if I had ever once thought of it. And I am only

too glad that this anomaly should have occurred
in my case, for, of a truth, it strikes me as much
greater as a metaphysical phenomenon than as
a juvenile virtue.*

In the very midst of my direst misfortunes,
when it seemed that nothing worse could possibly
happen to me, the Pacific came steaming back to
Detroit. She arrived in the afternoon, and, although I had had nothing to eat that day, I was
in too great apprehension of her captain to think
of anything but concealment, or escape from the
city.

After nightfall I stole on board the Michigan
Central steamer May Flower, and found the
fourth porter. I had been among menials so
long that I knew all about the ramifications of
their grades, and what particular line of duties
belonged to individuals of each grade. The
fourth porter, I was well aware, had charge of
the forecastle, where the deck-hands and firemen ate and slept.

* "Multum interest, utrum peccare aliquis nolit, aut nesciat."
This bit of Seneca seems so appropriate, that I hope the reader
will excuse me for quoting it here, even if I did get it at second-
hand from Montaigne.

Now the fourth porter of the May Flower was a lazy, good-natured little pock-marked Irishman, whom I had no great difficulty in persuading to smuggle me to Buffalo, on condition that I should do the greater part of his work in the forecastle. I was glad, it will be seen, to make any port in the storm which at that time swept across my terrified imagination ; Buffalo was not, of course, the best one for me, but anything seemed better, just then, than the prospect of that Cimmerian House of Vagrancy.

My friend, the fourth porter, was so well pleased with the skill and taste I displayed in the cleansing of his greasy dishes that he lent a degree of zeal to the carrying out of his part of the contract which wellnigh proved fatal to me. For, the next day, when we were out on the lake, and the fares were collecting, he hid me away between two mattresses, as black as the coal handled by the sturdy firemen who usually slept on them. I was already half smothered when the clerk and his satellites descended into the forecastle ; but the fourth porter, to crush out, I suppose, the merest crease of suspicion, sat down on the mattress which covered me, and carelessly picked his teeth till the danger was past.

It was well that the forecastle was so uninviting a place as to detain the clerk but a short time, since I should have screamed or perished in a half-minute more. When drawn out, at last, by the party of the first part to our contract, I was very black in the face, not only from the smothering I had endured, but from the coal-dust I had taken from the mattresses.

CHAPTER X.

ARRIVED safely at Buffalo, I did not look much like the urchin who had left there several months before. Although I had conscientiously washed my solitary piece of linen every week, and tried to keep myself as neatly as I could, my clothes were greasy and ragged and my boots nearly off my feet.

I wandered about the wharves without any purpose that I can now remember, and might have been very disconsolate if it were not for the joy I felt at escaping from the danger which I considered so imminent at Detroit. This latter city, indeed, I came to look upon as a peculiarly unlucky place for me, — an opinion which I continued to entertain up to the time of a signal triumph I had there afterward as the juvenile prodigy of jig-dancing and negro-minstrelsy.

I was just on the point of turning away from

the docks for a stroll up some of the neighboring squalid by-streets of Buffalo when I suddenly heard myself called by name. It would be hard to say when I was worse terrified. I was really afraid of my own name. No good could come to me, I felt sure, from any one's knowing it. Gazing around toward the wharf, in the direction from which the sound had seemed to come, I saw no-body but some laborers unloading a sailing vessel, close at hand, and they took no notice of me.

Again I heard my name, which sounded this time as if it came mysteriously from somewhere up in the air. Sweeping the dingy heights of the masts and smoke-stacks and office-windows with my astonished eyes, I beheld, at last, a boy com-ing briskly toward me down a flight of steps that led from a commission-house.

It was my school-fellow, who had harbored me in the stable the first night of my run-away ; and it was from the window of his father's office, he told me, that he had first seen and called me. "How you look ! but I am glad to see you !" and many other frank, kind things the generous little fellow said.

He prefaced his eager questions as to where I

had been and how I came to spoil my clothes so, with the remark that he guessed it was n't so funny, after all, to go out in the world seeking a fellow's fortune. My own plight at the time was better calculated, I think, than any moral observations I may have made, to fortify him in this opinion. If I did indulge in a few gravely eloquent words of warning, I have so far forgotten them that I cannot repeat them here for the benefit of thoughtless, adventure-loving boys of to-day.

As soon as I had briefly satisfied my friend's curiosity as to the dangers myself and clothes had passed, he insisted on my going right along home with him. I refused, of course, being ashamed of my toilet, and still afraid of capture by the people from whom I had fled. Whereupon my old school-mate assured me that his mother had scolded him for not before bringing me into the house instead of the stable. He gave me furthermore to understand that she had heard all about my domestic quarrel, and upheld me in what I had done.

This information had its effect, and I turned with him toward his home. The well-dressed

boy did not seem at all abashed to walk through
the most crowded streets with me, although the
striking contrast of our attire and social positions
must have been highly suggestive to any passing
philosopher.   Boys of the short-jacket age may,
by the way, have many imperfect and even cruel
traits, but we must confess, as men, that caste
begins on our side of long-tailed coats.

At my friend's home I received a kindly greet-
ing from his mother, who immediately insisted —
as good women in their hospitable souls often do,
for almost any ill that can befall a person — on
producing something to eat.   Now it happened,
for a wonder, that I was not hungry, having
scarcely an hour before taken a very hearty meal,
on general principles of prevention (though in
the middle of the forenoon), just previous to my
parting with the fourth porter of the steamer
May Flower.

But that did not satisfy the sympathy of my
friend's mother.   The hospitable longing just
hinted at, which not unfrequently seeks to administer consolation through the stomach for wounds
and sprains of the limbs as well as for wounds and

sprains of the heart and head, — the spirit which underlies, I suppose, the custom of funeral baked-meats, — was aroused in the kind-hearted lady. She saw, no doubt, in my stained and tattered garments an illuminated chronicle of present distress, and all manner of past misfortunes. And I had to eat again.

Then she sent me up stairs, and had me bathed and thrust into a suit of her son's clothes and a pair of his boots ; all of which fitted me admirably. Having changed my five pennies from the pocket of the old to that of the new pantaloons, I descended to meet her criticism. She seemed well pleased with the result, and, telling me I must take good care of the clothes and boots, for they were now mine, she made me sit down and give her an account of my wanderings. This ended, she dismissed me to play with her own boy, first making me promise I would come back to her house to eat and sleep.

My young friend, who had been an interested witness of my metamorphosis in all its stages, delighted, I need hardly add, as much as I did in his mother's benevolence, or as much as she did in our mutual joy. Indeed, the expression of the kind lady's face, calmly pleased at her own act, but brightly exultant in the reflection of our rejoicing, was then something beautiful to see, and has been grateful to think upon since. It was Saturday, and, there being no school, we two boys made a merry day of it, keeping, however, well out of the neighborhood of my former home.

I could not make my friend understand, any more than I can now myself, why I had not long before spent the five coppers he had given me. When I had plenty to eat they were, I remember, a kind of sword and shield to me, adding greatly to my independence, which almost always, at such moments of bodily fulness, was of the happy and triumphant sort. It was only in the seasons of my direst need that I had a vague expectancy of worse times; and against these worse times, I suppose, I held my coppers.

And the reader may explain, if he can, what is really the fact, that this apprehension of greater misfortunes than ever came — and which my pennies were sometimes powerless to dispel — and my fear of the heartless captain of the steamer Pacific were the only sources of unhappiness during my worst privations. If I could have been free of these, I am convinced, I might have been very hungry, but never very unhappy.

Over the supper-table that Saturday evening, my case and person having been made known to my friend's father, a consultation was had about my future. I was strongly in favor of going on a first-class steamboat, and rather forward, peradventure, in advocating my views. My friend's father, thinking of no better place for me to work for myself, or entertaining secret doubts as to my staying in any better place, if put there, promised his wife to see what he could do for me in the direction taken by my own inclinations.

Accordingly, on the next Monday, by his influence, and by the kindness of the late Captain Pheatt, a position was secured for me on the steamer Northern Indiana.

I received ten dollars a month for acting as what was called key-boy, whose light duties were to take care of the state-room keys and attend the steward's office. I had also the exclusive privilege of selling books and papers to the passengers. By favor I received a share of my wages in advance, and, adding my five coppers to the sum, I made my first investment in yellow-covered literature.

The steamer, which was a veritable floating palace, carried hundreds of passengers every trip, and I prospered. It was the custom of many people, in compliment to my diminutive size, or in disgust at their contents, to make me presents of their books, when they had read them, or tried to read them. Thus I had the good fortune to sell the same book two, three, and even four times over. I made ten and sometimes fifteen dollars a week in this way and in the legitimate merchandise of my books and papers.

Scarce seven moons from the time of my first flight from Buffalo, and my five coppers had increased to I know not how many dollars. When the steamer was laid up in the late autumn, I had money enough to keep me handsomely and send me to school all the next winter, — if, as shall be seen, fate, in the guise of disappointed affection, and a banjo, had not ordered otherwise.

It is just both to my natural and legal guardians to say here, that, when they saw me not only determined but able to support myself, they left

me ever afterward quietly to my own devices.
My necessities, therefore, and the prosperous result of my first adventures with five coppers, led
me to adopt — a little too romantically, perhaps,
in the latter and more thoughtful period of my
youth — a principle to which I long had a kindly
leaning, notwithstanding the hard knocks it dealt
me.   Indeed, it is still doubtful in my mind
whether it is not better to devote half of one's
energies in learning to live on a very small income than to devote all of one's energies in
struggling and waiting miserably for a very
large income.

   That, at least, was my principle; and, if it
trammelled the head with false doctrine, it left the
soul remarkably free.   Thus, it will be seen, my
entire subsequent wanderings, my course at an
American college, and at a German university —
the former on nothing to speak of, and the latter
on eighty dollars — all sprang more or less directly from the extraordinary qualities of expansion,
both spiritual and financial, which, at the early
age of eleven, I discovered in those five copper
cents.

BOOK II.

———◆———

THREE YEARS AS A NEGRO-MINSTREL.

ÆT. 12–15.

CHAPTER I.

NEGRO–MINSTRELS were, I think, more highly esteemed at the time of which I am about to write than they are now; at least, I thought more of them then, both as individuals and as ministers to public amusement, than I ever have since.

The first troupe of the kind I saw was the old "Kunkels," and I can convey no idea of the pleasurable thrill I felt at the banjo-solo and the plantation-jig. I resolved on the spot to be a negro-minstrel. Mr. Ford, in whose theatre President Lincoln was assassinated, was, I believe, the agent of this company. I made known my ambition to that gentleman and to Mr. Kunkel himself, and they promised, no doubt, as the best means of getting rid of me, to take me with them the next year.

Meantime I bought a banjo, and had pennies

screwed on the heels of my boots, and practised
"Jordan" on the former and the "Juba" dance
with the latter, till my boarding-house keeper
gave me warning. I think there is scarcely a
serious friend of mine acquainted with me at that
period who does not remember me with sorrow
and vexation. The racket that I made at all
hours and in all places can be accounted for only
by the youthful zeal with which I "practised,"
and which I despair of describing in anything so
cold as words.

I was then in my twelfth year, and my own
master. It was, indeed, in that prosperous winter after the squalid summer of my six months'
wandering. I was going to school at Toledo,
Ohio, and leading a very independent life on the
money I had made out of the common investment of my five coppers and of my wages, as key-
boy of the steamer Northern Indiana, commanded
by the late Captain Pheatt.

I mention this kindly old gentleman again in
the present connection because he suffered a
great deal from my early *penchant* to perform the
clog-dance on the thin deck above his state-room.
It is unnecessary to repeat here the eager and

emphatic remonstrances which the good captain would make when I had inadvertently seized the occasion of his "watch below" to shuffle him out of a profound sleep. But, I may remark in passing, I have never known any one who regarded everything about negro-minstrelsy with so little reverence or admiration.

It could not have been long after my interview with Messrs. Ford and Kunkel when my landlady gave me warning to take myself and banjo and obstreperous feet out of her house. With some difficulty, however, I found another place to board, where the plastering of the apartment below mine was proof against the coppers on my heels and the complicated shuffles of "Juba." For a month or two more I continued to go to school, devoting only my spare hours to minstrelsy. I should, no doubt, have abandoned my studies much sooner than I did, had it not been for a love-affair which for a while divided my attentions with my banjo.

My Dulcinea was a red-cheeked little creature in a check apron. I had a rival, in the same school with us, whom I vanquished by an unfair and lavish expenditure of my superior wealth. I used to get up foot-races for pennies in which

I contrived that her little brother should always beat and carry off the rewards. This was for a time effectual. My rival was completely ousted, and my two absorbing affections joined hands, as I may say figuratively, when the young lady and I met after school, in her father's wood-shed, and I played "Jordan" for her on the banjo.

She may have tired of my music, since that one tune executed mechanically was the alpha and omega of my repertory; or she may have tired of me, — I cannot speak definitely. If I had ever essayed to accompany the instrument with my voice, it would have been different. Then I never should have forgiven myself, and I could have forgiven her, after the *dénouement* which closed her heart and her father's wood-shed to me forever. For, in the course of a few brief weeks, a taller and much handsomer boy than either my former rival or myself took the little miss away from us both.

In my disgust, I left school and devoted all the energies of my blighted spirit to minstrelsy. I organized a band of boys into a troupe, styling them the "Young Metropolitans," and appointing myself musical director, though I knew no more of music than of chemistry. I spent my money for instruments for the company, and for furniture to deck the room in which we met for rehearsal. The musical instruments, however, were the least of the expense, since these consisted, if I well recollect, of the banjo before mentioned, three sets of bones, a tambourine, a triangle, and an accordion.

With these, nevertheless, we succeeded in making it very unpleasant for some quiet-loving Teutons who were accustomed to dream over their beer at a *Wirthschaft* in the same wooden building, and indeed just under the apartment in which we rehearsed every evening. On certain occasions, when I executed my "Juba" dance, or, in company with others, performed the Virginia walk-around, these honest Germans would leave their beer, and sometimes their hats and pipes, behind them in terror, and rush precipitately into the middle of the street. There they would stand and gaze in silent amazement up at the windows, or utter their surprise and wrath at the proceedings in the expressive, but unintelligible speech of the Fatherland.

5 *

The host, a portly gentleman with a red nose, remonstrated with us about four times a week, to little purpose. The owner of the building also remonstrated; but we had rented the apartment, and would not leave till our time was out. We were constrained, however, to forego our jig and walk-around. Still our music and singing, to which we were now confined, came near breaking up the poor retail Gambrinus of the saloon beneath. His "stem-guests" fell off one by one, and sought a quieter neighborhood for their evening potations. It was only the bravest of them that could be prevailed upon to return for anything more than their hats and pipes, after having been driven into the street on any of our siege-nights.

The best praise I can give to the young gentleman who played the accordion is, that he was worthy to be under such a musical director as myself. He could play only one tune from beginning to end, and that was the "Gum-Tree Canoe." Now it happened none of us could sing the song, which, as is well known, is of the slow, melancholy, sentimental order; so this single tune would have been of very little benefit to us, had we not, luckily, pressed it into the incongruous double service of opening overture and closing quickstep.

The songs that we sang, or attempted to sing, were executed to the accompaniment of the three sets of bones, the tambourine, triangle, and banjo, with an uncertain ghostly second on the accordion, which, being the same for all tunes and following no lead whatever, was of a sufficiently lugubrious and dismal nature, when it was not wholly drowned by the clangor of the other instruments.

My company, it must be confessed, had zeal, but little talent. I spent what was left of my summer's earnings before I could get them up to a point that would, in my judgment, warrant a hope of success, should we give the public exhibition for which my minstrels were clamorously ambitious.

After many long months of fruitless trial, the rent of our room becoming due, our furniture and instruments were seized ; the landlord turned us out of doors ; the German beer-seller crossed himself thankfully ; and I was as completely ruined as many a manager before me.

CHAPTER II.

I BECOME A BENEFICIARY.

IT may as well be owned that I had no natural aptness for the banjo, and was always an indifferent player ; but for dancing I had, I am confident, such a remarkable gift as few have ever had. Up to this day, I do not think I ever have seen a step done by man or woman that I could not do as soon as I saw it, — not saying, of course, how gracefully. I am not, however, so vain or proud of this gift as I used to be, and should hardly have written the foregoing sentence at all, had it not seemed necessary to a proper understanding of subsequent passages in this narrative.

I was still so small of stature, and yet capable of producing so much noise with the coppers on my heels, that, by the wholesale clerks and young bloods about town, I was considered in the light of a prodigy, and made to shuffle my feet at almost all hours and in almost all localities. It was by this means, at some place of convivial resort, that I attracted the notice and admiration of a conductor on the Michigan Southern and Northern Indiana Railroad. He determined to have so much talent with him all the time, and prevailed upon me to be his train-boy.

Here, as on the lake, I had the exclusive privilege of selling books and papers to the passengers. The great railways were not then farmed by a single person or firm as now. I was my own agent and the regulator of my own prices and profits. Both of these latter I found it convenient to make large, and was again the possessor of more money than I cared to spend.

It was my business to carry water through the cars at stated intervals. On a day train I could afford to perform my duty with promptness, when I had sufficiently worried the passengers with my merchandise. But on a night train — which came to my lot just as often as a day train — I took a more lucrative and, I fear, less reputable means of quenching the thirst of travellers. There were no sleeping-cars in those times, and, I believe, no water-tanks in the passenger-cars.

My memory may fail me in this matter of the water-tanks, but I am certain that I never filled them, if there were any on our road. I don't know whether more people travelled then than now, but I remember the trains were exceeding long ones in those hot summer nights, and the people became terribly thirsty. And this is the way I comforted them : —

Taking a barrel of water, a pailful of brown sugar, and a proper amount of a well-known acid, I concocted lemonade which I sold through the train for five cents a glass. When thirsty lips asked piteously for water, I would tell the sufferer, with perfect truth, that there was not a drop of pure water left on the train. I blush to write that I sometimes sold fifteen dollars' worth of this vile compound in a night.

I was taught how to prepare it by a man who travelled with a circus, and who assured me that all his ice-cold lemonade was concocted in the same way ; and that, far from having killed anybody, it gave perfect satisfaction to the gentlemen and ladies from the country, who were his principal customers.

The only excuse I have to offer for myself now

is, that I was not conscious then how great a villain I really was.

Toward the middle of the summer the cholera became so prevalent in the Western cities that I thought it prudent to retire from the active life of a train-boy, and live quietly on my earnings. I settled myself, therefore, at a fashionable boarding-house in Toledo.

Here the landlady, fearful of the dust and anxious for the integrity of her carpet, made a remarkable compromise with me to the glory of æsthetics. Whenever there was a pressing request from the boarders for me to exercise my feet, she would bustle in with a large roll of oil-cloth, and spread it uncomplainingly on the parlor floor near the piano to the music of which I danced. This was, I think, the first introduction of clogs as a drawing-room entertainment. I soon came to be invited out as a sort of cub-lion ; and thus it happened that the rumor and dust of my accomplishments spread gradually throughout the city.

One evening I strolled into what was then the St. Nicholas, and, stepping to the bar, which came just up to my juvenile shoulders, I demanded authoritatively of the bar-tender if he had any good pale brandy. He said that he had. I told him in the same imperative tone to give me a ten-cent drink, "and none of his instant-death kind either."

This made somewhat of a sensation among the frequenters of that fashionable resort. They evidently mistook this brandy-bibbing as a swaggering habit of mine ; whereas I was honestly prescribing for myself what had been recommended to me as the best preventive of cholera. Having swallowed and paid for the brandy, I was preparing to withdraw, when I heard this dialogue going on behind me : —

" Who for pity's sake is that ? "

" That ? why, that 's just the boy you want. But can't he dance though ! "

Turning, I saw a couple of well-dressed men seated together at the end of the room. I had barely time to observe that one was a stranger to me, when the other called me to him, and introduced me to Johnny Booker.

Now I had heard the songs, then popular, "Meet Johnny Booker in the Bowling Green," and

"Johnny Booker help dis nigger"; and when I was aware that I was standing before the person to whose glory these lyrics had been written, I was very much abashed. I looked upon a great negro-minstrel as unquestionably the greatest man on earth, and it was some time before I could answer his questions intelligibly.

In the course of a few minutes, however, I was conducted into a private room, where I was made to dance "Juba" to the time which the comedian himself gave me by means of his two hands and one foot, and which is technically called "patting." My performance, it seems, was satisfactory, for I was engaged on the spot.

Mr. Booker was then waiting for the rest of his company to join him; and when they arrived, I was instituted jig-dancer to the troupe, with a weekly salary of five dollars and all my travelling expenses.

The other performers came I know not from what dismembered bands, to the relief or grief of I know not what distant hotels or boarding-houses. But, I will venture to say, no landlord, to whom the more reckless of them may have been in arrears, could have regarded their movements with a more lively interest than I did, after their

H

arrival at Toledo.   As they came straggling in,
one after the other, with their bass-viols and gui-
tars and banjos in mysterious bags of green-baize
or glazed oil-cloth, I looked upon them as I might
have looked upon people who had come from
another world.

If some of them appeared a little seedy, in the
long interval between this and their previous engagement, and if others wore their coats strangely
buttoned over their shirt-bosoms, I put it down of
course to the peculiarity and privilege of genius.
When I walked through the streets to and from
rehearsal with these strange beings, it was a triumphal procession to me.   I seemed crowned for
the time with the glory with which my young
imagination had invested everything belonging
to them.

It is impossible to convey an idea of the gratified ambition with which I prepared for my first
appearance on the stage.   The great Napoleon in
the coronation robes, which can be seen any day
in the Tuileries, was not prouder or happier than I
when I made my initial bow before the foot-lights,
in my small Canton flannel knee-pants, cheap lace,
gold tinsel, corked face, and woolly wig.

I do not remember any embarrassment, for I was only doing in public what I had already done for the majority of the audience in private. If I had acquitted myself much worse than I really did, my *début* would still, I am convinced, have been considered a success.

So great, indeed, was the local pride of the good Toledans in their infant phenomenon, that after the company had exhibited a week, my name — or rather the *nom de guerre* which I had assumed — was put up for a benefit. On that day I had the satisfaction of seeing hung across the street, on a large canvas, a water-color representation of myself, with one arm and one leg elevated, in the act of performing "Juba" over the heads and carts and carriages of the passers-by.

At night the house was crowded, and I was called out three times ; but what afterwards struck me as unaccountably odd was, that I received not one cent from the proceeds of this benefit. When my salary was paid me, at the end of the next week, I was assured that "this benefit business" was a mere trick of the trade, and I was forced to content myself with the fact that I had learned something in my new profession.

CHAPTER III.

WE now started on our travels, staying from one night to a week in a city, according to its size, stopping always at the best hotels, and leading the merriest of lives generally. I had the additional glory of being stared at as the youthful prodigy by day, and of having more than my share of applause, accompanied sometimes with quarter-dollars, bestowed on me at night.

There are probably many who will yet remember to have seen their cities thoroughly posted and plastered with the glaring announcement, in gigantic red letters, that "The Metropolitan Serenaders" were "coming." That was our company, and in that golden age of minstrelsy our coming was an event of some importance. It certainly seemed so to the management; for on our arrival it was furthermore announced in large sky-blue letters, on all the prominent vacant buildings, and on all the low-tariff or free-trading board fences, that "The Metropolitan Serenaders" had "come."

Nor was this all. As soon as our property-boxes were unpacked, our portraits in most gorgeous colored daguerreotypes were suspended about the entrance to the hall where we were to perform, and about the reading-rooms of the principal hotels. Bad as these unquestionably were, they were the very perfection of that style of art in those days; and thus it happened that those even who came upon our pictures to scoff, remained to admire.

In addition, there was a collective and general — I may say, very general — representation of ourselves on canvas, suspended across the principal street; we being attired, for that pictorial occasion only, in green dress-coats and in pantaloons of the same shade as our lips, which were of a very brilliant and unnatural pink.

I was sometimes astonished at the stupidity of the common public, who would frequently, as I stood among them, in graceful incognito, point out on this superb water-color the picture of the guitar-player, and decide in my hearing that he must be meant for the "Juvenile Phenomenon."

Now this guitar-player was in reality the longest, lankest, and by all odds the homeliest man in the company ; and how the public should ever mistake him for me, the only original " Juvenile Phenomenon," was more than I could understand.

Looking back dimly through my memory at this picture, and aided as I am in my criticism by a recent interview with the venerable artist himself, I am led to conclude now, that he had idealized and etherealized the form of that tallest and ugliest of guitar-players. As represented on the canvas, " touching his light guitar," with his eyes turned upward in a Sapphic ecstasy, there was something so gigantically heroic in the spirit of his action, or in the blunder of the painter, that his body seemed in comparison to weigh but a scant ninety pounds, and all that was earthly in his appearance was, it must be owned, strikingly diminutive and phenomenal.

Notwithstanding the annoyance caused me by the mistake of the common public in the matter of identity, I do not wish to be unjust to our artist. He is still living, at Cincinnati, a gray-haired man, supporting a large family by the honorable exercise of his brush ; though of late years he has confined himself mostly, he assures me, to the more materialistic and lucrative branch of his profession, — house and sign painting, namely.

With regard to the picture in question, he said, the last time I saw him, that in it he had made an attempt, if he remembered correctly, to throw an ideal halo of high art about some of the portraits ; that the tall guitar-player was a special instance wherein this treatment seemed necessary ; and that, in all his artistic experience, he had never since come across a man that would stand so much foreshortening.

The latter part of the old painter's speech about the guitar-player was in a different tone of voice altogether, and in words which, from their queer pathos, I think I am reporting verbatim.

" Poor —— ! " he said, calling my old comrade by name ; " he has long since gone to his account. I suppose we must all go sooner or later." Then, after a meditative pause, the old fellow continued : " No man is homely, I guess, in heaven, or too long and bony for good proportion. They say, too, that there 's progression up there. He died more than ten years ago. Maybe he's now improving his talent by playing on a golden harp.

He was n't much of a guitar-player down here, but no matter."

There was in our troupe a remarkable character by the name of Frank Lynch, who played the tambourine and banjo. He and the celebrated Diamond had been in their youth among the first and greatest of dancers. Too portly now to endure sustained effort with his feet, he was yet an excellent instructor ; and I was constantly under his training.

He taught me, in addition to the legitimate sleights of our calling, to aid him in a droll way he had of amusing himself at the expense of the general public. He initiated me into the mysteries of beating the rolls and drags on the snare-drum ; and then it was our custom of a summer afternoon to steal away to the top of the hotel, or more generally to the roof of the hall where we were to exhibit. Placing ourselves so that we could observe the passers-by on the street, without being observed by them, Lynch would strike up a tune on the fife and I would accompany him on the drum ; and, straightway, the whole thoroughfare for a block or so in each direction would keep time to our music.

It was our delight to set our people all a going faster or slower, at our will. Curious persons would sometimes look about them, puzzled, to see where the music came from ; but, failing in that, they almost invariably marched on to some brisk or melancholy measure, as it chanced to be our mood at the moment. Any one who may doubt this statement has but to observe the foot-passengers the next time he or she hears a band of music playing on the street.

It would sometimes happen, however, that our notice would be attracted by the peculiar walk of an individual who had so little music in his soul that we could not bring him into step. In that case we would perform Mohammed's miracle of the mountain, by accommodating our fife and drum to his particular gait, and bring the rest of the street into the same pace.

If we saw an elderly gentleman or lady, Lynch would immediately launch forth into the well-known "limping tune" of the old man in the pantomime, and, as sure as fate, our venerable actor or actress below would keep time. The conventional air which heralds in Columbine on the Christmas boards was also brought into

6

requisition, with most remarkable effect, when we caught sight of a young lady or bevy of young ladies, promenading beneath us in spruce toilet.

On a hot day I am afraid we were sometimes a trifle cruel in the way we hurried up fleshy people. From our point of view on the roof, and generally behind a shady chimney, the effect was, in truth, not unlike that of a diorama. But especially was this the case when some stout old gentleman, whom we had precipitated along a whole block at a very lively, perspiring rate through a hot sun, would, as if melted or absorbed in the white light, disappear suddenly from our gaze, as a brisk and fiery execution of " The girl I left behind me " would carry him steaming around a corner.

In short, our martial music was an endless amusement to us when time hung heavy on the hands of the more dignified members of our company. By some accident, I forget what, we lost our small drum, and were afterward confined to a fife and a bass-drum. This, I think, only made the effect of our music more ludicrous in developing the peculiarities of individual pedestrians.

Lynch seemed, I remember, more than ever satisfied in this exigency, for he stoutly maintained
that any two faces are more alike than any two
"gaits," and that, for his part, he always wanted the
top of a house, a fife, and at least a bass-drum to
read character.

Lynch and I were together in another troupe
afterward. I never knew him, in all the time of
our association, to talk ten minutes without telling some story, and that always about something
which had happened to him personally in the
show business. In the long nights, when we had
to wait for cars or steamboats, he would sit down,
and, taking up one theme, would string all his
stories on that, and that alone, for hours. His
manner would make the merest commonplace
amusing.

We had been together a year or more, I think,
when Barnum's Autobiography came out. I shall
never forget my comrade's indignation when he
read that passage of the book which runs something in this way : " Here I picked up one Francis
Lynch, an orphan vagabond," &c., &c. It was
really dangerous after that for a man to own, in
his presence, to having read the life of the great

showman. Henceforth, Lynch omitted all his stories about the time when he and P. T. Barnum used to black their faces together.

Lynch professed to live in Boston, though he had not been there in fifteen years. During all this time he had been earnestly trying to get back to his home. He would often spend money enough in a night to take him to Boston from almost any place in the broad Union, and back again, and then lament his folly for the next week.

Once he left our company at Cleveland, Ohio, for the express purpose of going back to Boston. Unfortunately a night intervened, and in the middle of it the whole Weddell House was aroused from its slumbers by poor Lynch, in the last stage of intoxication, vociferating at the top of his lungs that he had been robbed of the money with which he was going back to Boston.

By some means he had got hold of a lighted candle without a candlestick, and with this he purposed to search the house. The clerks and porters were called out of bed, and, led by Lynch with his flickering taper, came in melancholy procession up the long stairs to the rooms occupied by our troupe. Lynch insisted that we should all be searched, — a whim in which, under the circumstances, we thought it best to humor him. This having been done without finding his lost treasure, he bolted the doors and proceeded to examine the surprised clerks and porters. Meeting with the same ill success, he finally threw himself in despair upon his bed, and wailed himself to sleep.

The next morning he found all the money which he had not spent in the side pocket of his overcoat, where he had carelessly thrust it himself. And his joy was so great at this, and his sorrow so lively when told that he had searched us all, that he insisted on spending what money was left to celebrate his good luck and the triumph of our honesty.

Lynch never got back to Boston. He died several years ago somewhere out in the far West. Since then it has transpired that Barnum was wrong in calling him an orphan, at least ; for his father sought him a long time before hearing of his death, to bestow upon the poor fellow a considerable fortune that had been left him by some relative.

Johnny Booker was the stage-manager of the company with which I left Toledo. Our first business-manager and proprietor was a noble-hearted fellow, who has since distinguished himself as a colonel in the late war; but the manager-ship changed hands after a while, and we finally arrived at Pittsburg. Here we played a week to poor houses, and, one morning, awoke to find that our manager had decamped without paying our hotel bills.

When this became known, through the papers or in some other way, the landlord got out an attachment on our baggage. The troupe was disbanded, of course. When, therefore, I desired to take my trunk and go home, the hotel-keeper told me that I could do so as soon as I paid the bills of the whole company. This was appalling.

After a great deal of wrangling, the landlord was convinced at last that he could hold us responsible only for our individual indebtedness. Accordingly Mr. Booker, Mr. Kneeland, a violinist, and myself were allowed to pay our bills and depart with our baggage.

I never learned exactly how the greater part of

the company escaped, but it certainly could not have been by discharging their accounts; for they were generally of that reckless disposition which scorns to have any cash on hand, or to remember where it has been deposited.

The sentimental ballad-singer, — the one who was the most careful of his scarfs, the set of his attire, and the combing and curling of his hair; and who used to volunteer to stand at the door in the early part of the evening, and pass programmes to the ladies as they came into the hall, — this languishing fellow, I am sorry to say, was obliged to leave his trunks and the greater part of his wardrobe behind him in the hands of the inexorable landlord.

Frank Lynch had led this nomadic life so long that he never carried any trunk with him. He had already sacrificed too much, he averred, to the rapaciousness of hotel-keepers and the villany of fly-by-night managers. He contented himself, therefore, with two champagne-baskets, one of which, containing his stage wardrobe, always went directly to the hall where we were to play, while the other, containing his linen, went to the hotel, where, in company with the baggage of the whole troupe, it excited no suspicion.

Whether or not Lynch left one of his champagne-baskets with the Pittsburg landlord I cannot say. I am sure, however, when we met afterward, I could not detect that his wardrobe had diminished in the least. Indeed, there was this remarkable quality about the two champagne-baskets, in which the convivial peripatetic may be said to have lived, that their contents never seemed either to diminish or increase.

CHAPTER IV.

THE TRIALS AND TRIUMPHS OF THE "BOOKER TROUPE."

THE two gentlemen with whom I left Pittsburg accompanied me to Toledo, where Mr. Booker set to work to get up another company. It was not long till we heard of Lynch at Cincinnati in search of an engagement, and he was accordingly sent for. Mr. Edwin Deaves, also a member of the defunct "Serenaders," — and now, by the way, a gray-haired wood-engraver and scenic artist at San Francisco, — was brought from some other place, and the "Booker Troupe" set out on its travels.

This company prided itself on its sobriety and gentlemanly conduct. It was the business of the four other members to keep poor Lynch straight, and if, in the endeavor, some of them occasionally fell themselves, it was put down to the reckless good-fellowship of the merry veteran, and hushed up as expeditiously as possible.

6 *   1

There were so few of us that we could afford to go to smaller towns than the other troupe had ever visited. It was deemed a good advertisement, as well as in some metaphysical way conducive to the *morale* of the company, to dress as nearly alike as we could when off the stage. This had the effect, as will be readily understood, of pointing me out more prominently than ever as the juvenile prodigy whose portrait and assumed name were plastered about over the walls of the towns and cities through which we took our triumphal march.

The first part of our performances we gave with white faces, and I had so improved my opportunities that I was now able to appear as the Scotch girl in plaid petticoats, who executes the inevitable Highland Fling in such exhibitions. By practising in my room through many tedious days, I learned to knock and spin and toss about the tambourine on the end of my forefinger; and, having rehearsed a budget of stale jokes, I was promoted to be one of the "end-men" in the first part of the negro performances.

Lynch, who could do anything, from a solo on the penny trumpet to an obligato on the double-bass, was at the same time advanced to play the second violin, as this made more music and helped fill up the stage.

In addition to my jig, I now appeared in all sorts of *pas de deux*, took the principal lady part in negro ballets, and danced "Lucy Long." I am told that I looked the wench admirably. Indeed, I have always considered it a substantiation of this fact, rather than an evidence of his maudlin condition, that a year or so subsequently a planter in one of the Southern States insisted on purchasing me from the door-tender, at one of our exhibitions. The price he offered and the earnestness and apparent good faith in which he offered it were so flattering that I have always regretted the necessity in which the door-tender at last considered himself, of kicking that planter down stairs.

The "Booker Troupe" wandered all over the Western country, travelling at all hours of night and day and in all manner of conveyances, from the best to the worst. The life was so exciting, and I was so young, that I was probably as happy as an itinerant mortal can be in this world of belated railway-trains, steamboat explosions and collisions, and runaway stage-horses.

In the smaller cities and towns we would sometimes, " by particular request," end up the evening with a ball. While we were washing the burnt cork from our faces, the ushers would remove the seats, and for a certain fee those ladies and gentlemen who delighted in the dance were readmitted to the hall. Then the four adults of the troupe, attired in their very best " citizens' dress," as they called it, would discourse music for the dancers.

My musical incompetency was at these times a signal advantage to me, for I was left free to go into society. I danced a great deal and with considerable *éclat*, on such occasions. My salary, which increased gradually with my progress in the " profession," was at this period squandered almost entirely upon my back. I was under the impression that my importation of metropolitan cuts and fashions into those provincial places was something altogether killing. My jewelry, if I remember well, was just simply astonishing for a boy of my age.

From these towns where we had dancing-parties I always went away with love-affairs on my hands. The amount of gold rings which I exchanged with young ladies between the ages of eleven and thirteen years was, to say the least, extraordinary.

Sunday in a small city is generally a heavy day with your minstrel. He writes to his wife, if he has any, or, if he has none, he practises solos on the bass-viol or some other instrument that ought never to be played solo, or yawns or lounges about the common room of the company. I used to pass these days, I am sorry to say, in replying to voluminous, ill-spelt correspondence from young persons with whom I had danced, a week or so back ; and if I happened to have a flame in the same town, I would go to church with the very reprehensible motive of seeing her, or walking home with her.

I ought to have known that this was highly improper conduct, even if the simple appearance of a negro-minstrel at church had not almost invariably produced great scandal to the congregation. I am glad, however, to be able to add that my toilet and behavior in such places were always scrupulously careful.

I do not know whether it is quite seemly in me to tell of it, but during the past winter I had occasion to lecture in a town which had once been the scene of one of these erotic exploits ; and there were sitting in a row on a front seat in the audience not only the quondam heroine and the gentleman who has for many years been her husband, but her father and mother, and, worst of all, that · brother of hers who intercepted our letters and who had threatened profanely to "punch" my "head." Now, although our attachment had been of the most harmlessly juvenile kind, the reader will imagine my embarrassment when I had the honor of an introduction to this whole family, and when the past was talked over by them in the most ruthlessly philosophical manner.

At a certain county-seat in Michigan the " Booker Troupe" had a remarkable bout with a moral editor. There must be many persons in that county, especially of the legal fraternity, who yet remember at least the catastrophe of the strange affair. This is the way it happened, as nearly as I can recall it : —

There were two weekly papers published in

that town at the time. Our agent had given our advertisement to one of these papers, and the other without authority had copied it. When the bills were brought to be paid, that of the paper which had printed our advertisement without warrant was about three times as much as the regular price, or as the other paper had charged. To Mr. Booker's remonstrance it was answered that the exorbitant bill must be paid, that shows were immoral things anyway, and that it was the purpose of that particular weekly newspaper to put them down. This was the moral editor who spoke.

Mr. Booker offered him the same amount that the other paper had charged, and bluntly refused to give a cent more. The moral editor would not take a cent less than his first charges, and, in default of immediate payment, would get out an attachment.

Now the constable, in common with most of the citizens, sympathized with Mr. Booker. In fact, the red nose and generally dissipated air of the moral editor made decidedly against the honesty of his intentions as a missionary of reform. And thus it happened, by some intentional delay in the making out of the papers, that the constable and the creditor arrived at the station to attach our baggage just at the time when it was all carefully stowed away in the baggage-car, and when the train was moving off with us on board.

The editor in great rage, notwithstanding his mission as moral censor, indulged in a great deal of profanity, by way of making it the better understood that he would follow us to the ends of the earth, — as soon as he could get the proper warrant made out.

Our next stopping-place was a brisk little town which chanced to be in the same county. We exhibited there and slipped away to our next point on a midnight train, leaving Mr. Booker behind to encounter the attachment, which, from private advices, we were led to expect the following morning. The officer accosted Mr. Booker as he was getting on the train, and asked him if an old weather-beaten valise which he carried in his hand was his. It was ; and that was all the baggage he had with him, the rest having gone on, of course, with us by the night train.

With imposing formality the old weather-beaten valise was attached. The key was also given up,

I do not know whether to the officer or to a lawyer who had come up from the county-seat to advise us in the matter. The lawyer then and there, in the presence of the officer and of the interested spectators, was intrusted formally with the case, and, Mr. Booker joining us in a few hours there-after, we proceeded unmolested on our travels.

The justice and the counsel on both sides seem to have entered into the affair with the design of getting all the sport they could out of it. On the day of the trial the court-room was thronged. In the absence of witnesses for the defence, and I suppose also by collusion, the case went against the " Booker Troupe." The editor, who was of course present, was in great glee.

At this stage of the proceedings it has been related — I know not how truly — the Justice arose, and in the most solemn manner spoke of the case as peculiarly aggressive on the part of a company of itinerant showmen; and inas-much as their fellow-citizen had taken it upon himself, single-handed, to drive this growing evil out of the land, therefore the magistrate ordered, although it was a little informal, that the consta-ble without further delay, which had in the tardy course of justice been too long already, should in the presence of that court open the valise and proceed to the sale of its contents.

The face of the moral editor is reported to have beamed more brightly than ever at this stage of his triumph.

With much pomp and circumstance the key was produced, and the ragged valise brought forward and opened. As nearly as I can remember, from having been present at the packing, and from an account of the affair sent to us afterward, the constable then began with grave deliberation to draw forth from that discouraged old portmanteau the following articles, to wit :-

1 large brick,

1 quart of beans,

1 silk hat, without rim or lining,

3 lbs. potatoes, — which latter had sprouted in the delays of justice,

1 old boot,

1 letter of congratulation to the moral editor, — which was read in open court, —

And, worst of all, 1 life-size wood-cut representation of Mr. Booker himself, with an old valise in one hand and a superannuated umbrella in the other, as he was wont to appear in his wonderful plantation act of "The Smoke-house Reel."

During the slow exposure of each of these articles, one after the other, there was some attempt to keep order in court, but by the time the last one was reached even the attempt was abandoned. The scene became uproarious, and the court was adjourned.

The moral editor never heard the last of it. He was forced to sell out his reformatory newspaper and leave the town.

We were on our way east from Chicago, exhibiting at the towns along the line of the Michigan Central Railroad, when Ephraim came to us. Ephraim was one of the most comical specimens of the negro species. We were playing at Marshall, Michigan, when he introduced himself to our notice by bringing water into the dressing-room, blacking our boots, and in other ways making himself useful.

He had the blackest face, largest mouth, and whitest teeth imaginable. He said there was nothing in the world which he would like so well as to travel with a show. What could he do?

Why, he could fetch water, black our boots, and take care of our baggage. We assured him that we could not afford to have a servant travel with us. Ephraim rejoined that he did not want any pay ; he just wanted to go with the show. We told him it was simply impossible ; and Ephraim went away, as we thought, discouraged.

The next morning, as we were getting into the railway-car, whom should we discover there before us but Ephraim, with his baggage under his arm, — a glazed travelling-bag of so attenuated an appearance that it could not possibly have had anything in it but its lining. To the question as to whither he was bound he replied, " Why, bless you, I 's goin' wid de show." Again he was told that it could not be, and made to get out of the car.

This occurrence gave Mr. Lynch the theme for a long series of stories about people he had met, who were what he called "show-struck"; and with these narratives our time was beguiled till we reached the town at which we were to perform that night. As we walked out towards the baggage-car, what was our surprise to see Ephraim there, picking out and piling up our trunks, and bestowing sundry loud and expressive epithets upon the baggage-master, who had let a property-box fall upon the platform.

I think we laughed louder now than we had at any of Mr. Lynch's stories. Ephraim deigned not to notice us or our mirth, but, having picked out the baggage that went to the hall where we were to exhibit, he called a dray and rode away with it.

He made himself of great use during our stay in that place, in return for which his slight hotel expenses were paid ; but he was told positively that he could go no farther. We knew that he had no money, yet did not dare to give him any, lest he should be enabled to follow us to the next town. So, when we came to go away, we expressed our regrets to the ingenuous darky, and once more bade him good by. He disappeared in the crowd, and the train moved off.

When we arrived at the next town, however, there again was Ephraim, at the baggage-car, giving his stentorian commands about our trunks and properties, and taking not the least notice of the surprise depicted on our faces.

The discharge and mysterious reappearance of

Ephraim occurred in about the same manner at
every town along the road until we reached Detroit.   We never could find out how he got from
place to place on the cars ; but where our baggage was, there was Ephraim also.   We had to
succumb.   His persistency and faithfulness and
perfect good-nature carried the point ; and he became a regular *attaché* of the " Booker Troupe."

The story of the fights and beatings that poor
Ephraim sustained in his jealous care of our lug-
gage would alone make a long chapter.   He was
always at fisticuffs with the Irish porters of the
hotels.   On one occasion, when remonstrated with
for his excessive pugnacity, Ephraim explained
himself in this way : " For one slam of a trunk I
gen'lly speaks to a man ; for two slams I calls
him a thief ; and when it comes to three slams,
den dere 's gwine to be somebody knocked down.
Now you heered me ! "

On our arrival at the hotel in Detroit we
observed that the porter was an Irishman, and
were really surprised that he and Ephraim did
not quarrel in handling the baggage, — an
anomaly which was satisfactorily explained to
us afterward, by the fact that the porter had

lately come to this country, and was, moreover, only about half witted. Now Ephraim was in the habit of taking his meals in the kitchens, and of sleeping in whatever attic was assigned him. On our first night in Detroit he had been sent into the servants' chamber, somewhere in the topmost part of the hotel. Ephraim ascended, disrobed himself, and, with his usual recklessness, got into the first of the many beds he saw in the large room.

At twelve o'clock, when his watch was over, the Irish porter also proceeded to the same apartment, with the purpose of retiring. Opening the door, he discovered by the dim gaslight something dark on the pillow of his own bed. This brought all his Old-World superstition into play in a moment. Going as much nearer as he dared, he saw that it was a black head, and, believing firmly that the Devil was black, he was sure that the Devil was in his bed.

The affrighted porter gave an unearthly yelp, at which Ephraim started up in terror. Whereupon the Irishman seized one of the negro's boots from the floor by the foot of the bed, and fell to beating the supposed Devil over the head

with all his might. The attack was so sudden
that Ephraim never thought of defence, but,
springing to his feet, fled precipitately down the
six flights of stairs, out into the middle of the
street, crying, "Watch, watch!" at the top of
his voice. Here a policeman came along, and
took poor Ephraim off to the station-house just
as he was, and in spite of all his protestations of
innocence.

The next morning Mr. Booker carried his
clothes to the unfortunate negro, and brought
him back to the hotel.

CHAPTER V.

IN the course of time the "Booker Troupe" was disbanded, and Ephraim, as well as ourselves, was, in green-room parlance, out of an engagement. I never saw him or Lynch afterward. Mr. Edwin Deaves, as I have intimated, is an industrious maker of wood-cuts and painter of transparencies and theatrical illusions in San Francisco. He was the gentlemanly "middle man" and barytone of this company. I never met him professionally after our disbanding. He went to California, I believe, with the late Samuel Wells, in the same troupe with Messrs. Birch and Backus.

Deaves was a very handsome man in the old days of our association. His jet-black hair never required a wig at that time, except when he desired to personate some terrible *impresario* in burlesque opera. Then he would invest himself in one of buffalo-robe, and would roar with such unexampled fierceness that our tin horns would ring again with the mere echoes of his powerful voice.

He was a man of great versatility. I would not like to say exactly what he could not do, from the invention of a patent soap to the plotting of a new pantomime. The words and music of some of the most widely known of the old negro melodies are of his composition.

But as I saw him last with his large family around him, at San Francisco, it was evident that, if he should ever go back from his present contented, peaceful life into the checkered uncertainties of cork opera, he would have to wear a wig, unless he confined himself exclusively to "old man's parts." His hair has long since faded, and he would, I fear, have also to use a tin horn himself, to produce the startling echoes of his whilom unaided voice.

With Mr. Kneeland, the violinist and musical director of the " Booker Troupe," I travelled subsequently in two other companies. As I shall have no occasion to mention him again, I

will say here that he was a quiet, modest sort
of fellow, who had a remarkable talent for sleeping. That man could sleep at any time and in
any place. If he happened to be forgotten in
the hurry of changing conveyances, — which was
not infrequently the case, — he was sure to be
left snoring in some waiting-room, or crouched
down among the cushions in some railway coach,
with his violin-box for a pillow.

He alone always played for my jigs and horn-
pipes; and as I used to get a side view of him on
the stage, with his eyes shut and his heel beating
the measure of the ecstasy which at such moments travelled, for instance, " The rocky road to
Dublin," away up into the cirrus heaven of the
octaves, I was more than once impressed with
the annoying belief that he was asleep, or soon
would be, and that I should have to complete my
grand *finale* of wings and shuffles to the uncertain
fugue of his snoring.

Whether he ever did fall asleep or not on the
stage I cannot tell for sure ; but, asleep or awake,
he always managed to keep better time than
I did.

He practised De Bériot's " Seventh Air " for

six months almost constantly in his room, never
to my knowledge venturing to play it in public.
Now his room was generally the next one to mine,
and I have often wished, after three or four steady
hours of De Bériot, that Mr. Kneeland would fall
asleep; yet by a strange fatality he never did,
unless there was some likelihood of his being left
behind.

Nevertheless, Kneeland was, by all odds, the
best-natured and the most substantial man of
the "Booker Troupe." He is now, I hear, the
thrifty and honest possessor of a goodly farm in
Wisconsin, where he lives with his wife and children. Of late years, it is only when the crops are
poor or the monotony of rural pursuits leaves him
open to the temptation, that he abandons his
plough, like another sturdy Cincinnatus, to give
his services to the public. Then for a brief summer he will, it is said, sally forth to lead the
brass and string band of some circus or menagerie to the conquest of bucolic or urban ears,
and fractional currency.

After a whole season of ovations, in which captive elephants and camels and lions, or superb
band-wagons and "grand entries" and bare-back

equestrians, have moved to the time of his music, the honest Kneeland goes back to his cows and sheep and domestic hearth, and is happy.

Johnny Booker still lives. I meet him every few years in the most out-of-the-way and unexpected places. He confines himself now, I believe, exclusively to the circus or menagerie business. One or the other branch of this style of tent-life seems, by the way, to be the ultimate refuge of your old showman, — the last stage of his worldly transmigrations.

Some seasons I will come across Mr. Booker in the very heart of this continent, convulsing a rural community with the sparkling manner in which he will answer, as clown, to the conventional, " This way, Mr. Merryman ; ask the young lady what she will have now." At other seasons and on the remotest rim of our territorial possessions, I will be astonished to recognize him in the magniloquent ring-master who inflicts the lashes upon the painted clown, and who acts the part of the Greek chorus, explaining the jokes of that amusing fellow in the choicest Doric of our language.

I have even known him to deliver a moral and instructive lecture on the nature and habits of the elephant, in a "grand combination" menagerie. Indeed, it was his custom, every afternoon and evening, to discourse on this branch of natural history when I last met my old friend and instructor in minstrelsy. He took great interest in his elephant, and especially in a living hippopotamus, which was the ruling attraction of his establishment,—just as he had once, I am bound in gratitude to say, taken great interest in me.

My place as his pupil was just then usurped by a small Irish lad, whom he pointed out to me, in an expansive feminine wig of flaxen curls and in puerile tights and tunic, with a most formidable gold-foil battle-axe in one hand, and the American flag in the other; personating, as Mr. Booker assured me, a water-nymph, on the silver-scaled but somewhat shaky chariot of Neptune.

This imposing car of the sea-god, I need scarcely add, formed part of the procession as it entered town, headed by the elephant, the living hippopotamus, and a brass-band seemingly on the point of death, so red and distended was the face

of each strangling musician, and so nearly did
each appear to have "poured through the mellow
horn his pensive soul."

The procession was still passing the balcony of
the hotel on which we were standing, when Mr.
Booker confided to me very gravely that his present pupil did not give him satisfaction. "He
will never be a performer," said the thoughtful
veteran ; "I don't know what I *can* make of that
boy, for," pursued Mr. Booker, with his mind
evidently more upon his pupil than upon me, —
"for I don't think he is even fit to write books."

My former manager at this moment became
so suddenly absorbed in the contemplation of a
large spot on the very masculine tunic of his
charge, the water-nymph, that he did not notice
how frank he had been with me. It is due, however, to the magnanimity of Mr. Booker to say,
that, whatever may be his private opinion of literature and of my change of profession, we are,
and I hope always shall be, the most devoted
of friends.

Whenever we meet he is sure to startle me
with a new batch of reminiscences of our old-time
companionship. What puzzles me most is that, as

he advances in years, his accounts of my youthful exploits grow more extended and apocryphal.
He has long since in these narratives got out of
the horizon of my memory. I would not for the
world accuse my old instructor of a want of candor, but I must say I think he has confounded
me with other and later of his pupils.

It would be as useless as ill-mannered to con-
tradict him, for he has told these stories so often
that he believes them implicitly himself. Any
unbiassed mind, moreover, will find excuse for the
treachery of his memory in the devious and exciting course of his subsequent life, as corypheus
of the saw-dusty ring, and especially as the zo-
ologist of the living hippopotamus, and as the
moral lecturer upon the manners and customs of
the elephant.

I shall, however, in closing this account of the
" Booker Troupe," give a couple of condensed
samples which will, I think, of themselves explain
why I indulge in no more of Mr. Booker's stories
about myself. I give them as a simple act of justice to my old comrades. Having related my
reminiscences of them with great freedom, it is no
more than fair that one of them, at least, should
be heard against me.

While admitting that a boy of thirteen may not have all the discretion in the world, still I herewith enter the solemn protest of my memory against the facts of the following statements.

Mr. Booker says that in the course of our travels we came to a city where I had relatives, and that I took occasion, as the best means of impressing them with my prosperity and independence, to appear in a different suit of clothes as often as I visited them, which was two or three times a day.

He furthermore relates with appalling circumstantiality, that at a select "hop" after our performances in some quiet little city, my attention was attracted by a very pretty young lady who seemed to be the belle of the evening. With the interested swagger of a young blood of thirteen years, I asked who that "fine girl" was. I was told that she was a certain Miss So-and-so, whom, for the sake of Mr. Booker's story, we will call Miss Brown ; and that she was of a very respectable family in that city.

Now it happened in the course of our wanderings that, from motives of curiosity, charity, and advertisement combined, we always visited the

7 *

state-prisons which chanced to be in our route, and sang and played to the prisoners, generally while they were assembled at dinner. And I may add here, by way of parenthesis, that never elsewhere have I witnessed so wonderful an illustration of the power of music as greeted us on such occasions. Hundreds would change from laughter to tears, and from tears to laughter again, as the song or strain was merry or sad. Two or three weeks before the time of Mr. Booker's story we had, he says, visited one of these prisons, and we had all become very much interested in the case of a handsome young fellow who had just been brought there for some crime committed while under the influence of liquor.

As soon as I heard the young lady's name, I remembered all about this unfortunate young fellow; and, especially, that he bore the same surname and came originally from that very town, although he had been convicted in another State. I found by inquiry that she, the handsome young lady, and life of the whole company, was the sister of the criminal. It was very plain that she had not yet heard of her brother's misfortune.

Then, according to Mr. Booker's account, I

obtained an introduction to her ; and, boy-like, in the honest but inconsiderate delight of being the first to bear her news which she, doubtless, would want to hear, I said, — "Miss Brown, Miss Brown, your brother's in the penitentiary!"

The young lady swooned, of course, and was borne home by her friends.

Mr. Booker always adds, at this place, that I ought to have been taken out and thrashed, — an opinion in which I should agree heartily if I did not doubt the truth of the whole story.

CHAPTER VI.

"THE MITCHELLS."

DURING the time I was waiting for another engagement I wandered to a large Western city, and took board in a respectable private family. There were three unmarried daughters in this household, the youngest of whom could not, I think, have been less than twenty-six years old. Notwithstanding the disparity of our ages, my memory is very much at fault if I was not in love with all three of these ladies at once. Nothing else, at least, could account to me now for the regularity with which I conducted this mature trio to theatres and concerts. From their readiness to go four and five evenings a week, I am also led to conclude that they individually and collectively encouraged my suit.

What names these three weird sisters bore, and how they looked, are matters which have long since escaped me; but the alacrity with which

they would go to ice-cream saloons in the afternoon, or to places of amusement in the evening,
at my expense, made such an impression on my
purse at the time that I have not forgotten it, as
you see, to this day.

I know not in what this state of affairs would
have ended, had it not been for a professional
engagement tendered me in the midst of my prod-
igality. Before leaving that city, I have a faint
remembrance of having formed one of a band of
two or three who undertook to furnish the amusement for a " Grand Gift Enterprise."

Finally I found myself, after some minor adventures, at Cincinnati, where the once notorious
Mike Mitchell left the Campbell's Minstrels and
took me with him into a company which he organized there, under the title of " The Mitchells." We played some time at the largest hall
in Cincinnati, boarding the while at the Gibson
House.

At this hotel I became acquainted with a
chubby, handsome boy, about as tall as I was, who
excited my admiration in an extraordinary manner. He would go to the theatre or some place of
amusement every evening, and nevertheless get

up at four or five o'clock every morning. I burned with a desire to wrestle with that boy.

This occurred to me as the only way to gratify my curiosity and establish a droll theory I had that any lad who could do with so little sleep must be a young giant. At last I inveigled him into my room, and the greater part of my remaining days in Cincinnati were spent in that cheerful and invigorating style of contest, to the no little damage of the furniture and our clothes, and of the nerves of a rheumatic old bachelor who occupied the apartment just under us.

There could have been nothing of the giant in the boy, after all, since we were so evenly matched. And, somehow, my belief in his wonderful sleeplessness was sadly dissipated. Whether he subsequently told me himself, or I found out by personal observation, I have forgotten; but I learned at last to account for his power of early rising in a way only less remarkable than the physical endurance of which I had thought him capable.

This young gentleman, it seems, was in the habit of going to sleep in his seat at the theatre, just after the overture by the orchestra. What struck me as particularly astonishing was that he always had the faculty of waking up when the dancing and comic songs came in, and especially when the broadsword and other combats took place. A tragedian never died to slow music in his presence but the young gentleman's critical eye, refreshed and sharpened by recent repose, was upon him.

In a word, whatsoever the act or scene in which it occurred, my young friend was always "in at the death." And he seemed to know by instinct, without consulting a ponderous gold watch which he carried, when it was time for the play to end.

Thus, it will be seen, he went away from the theatre with his night's rest already half complete, and was able to arise at four or five the next morning and deliver to any chance comer throughout the day a reliable opinion on the best points made the evening previous by Jamison or Murdoch — the actors of those times — in the great scene wherein Macduff "lays on"; or this young gentleman could tell you, perhaps, the number of times the blades struck fire in the mighty broadsword battle, sustained single-handed against fearful odds, by Mrs. Wilkinson in the "French Spy."

In the course of time our company started on its travels through the neighboring States, and when we returned to Cincinnati, my young friend and fellow-wrestler was gone ; moved away with his parents from the hotel, I was told, and to another city.

Now what has made this reminiscence especially interesting, at least to me, was my next meeting with the subject of it, years and years afterward ; because that was one of the strange occurrences which are, after all, about as frequent in an adventurous life as they are in fiction.

At a little inn in the shadow of the Odenwald, not far from the Rhine, I had the pleasure of taking him the next time by the hand. We have since passed many a day together on the Iser and Seine and Tiber, and we have slept many a night in the most uninviting of *auberges* and *Gasthäuser;* and not there, I am proud to say or in his hospitable mansion on Michigan Avenue, or, late at night, in the office of the great newspaper which he helps to edit, have I ever, in his generous manhood, discovered any sleeping on his post, or sleeplessness off from it.

There were in " The Mitchells " more discordant elements than I recollect to have known in any other troupe in the fortunes of which I ever had a part. I think there were too many leading comedians and musical stars among us for anything so sober and dull as a good understanding to exist at all times.

Some one, you know, must play second parts and second violin ; and that necessity was a smothered volcano in our midst. Stale jokes, unuttered, sit heavily on your comedian's memory ; they must be refreshed or renewed by the laughter of an audience ; and eclipsed musical brilliancy, when turned in upon itself, illumines a very disagreeable void, and generally results in heart-burnings.

I have a lingering impression that I myself, in this company, sighed regretfully for my old place as tambourinist and end-man. There were three other tambourinists and end-men who, like myself, had been professionally cut short in a comic career, to make way for a person whose jokes, in our opinion, were not half so good as ours, and for whose acrobatics with the complicated tambourine itself we were united, as three men and one boy, in our sublime contempt.

K

We had as musical director a very young Italian, who had led the orchestra of the Grand Opera at Havana, and he managed to lead our musicians into the most unconscionable difficulties and misunderstandings. I cannot conceive how in the world he did it, but he had them continually by the ears.

At one rehearsal there was such a jealous *mêlée* that a veteran violinist, an irascible old German, was forced to leave his wig behind him on the stage and retreat precipitately, with no more hair on his head than there is on a hairdresser's block. Indeed, as his smooth occiput disappeared through the dressing-room door, it resembled nothing so much as a back view of one of those familiar ornaments of a wig-maker's window.

The business manager of this company was a character that has puzzled me a great deal, — a human riddle that I solve a new way every time I attempt it. The last solution, too, is always sure to be just contrary to the one immediately preceding.

The name of this moustached Sphinx was "Governor" Dorr, or that, at least, was the name he went under. How he got, or what right he had to, either his title or surname I do not know. He had gambled for thousands in California, and been an adventurer in every land. He knew Shakespeare, seemingly, by heart. His common conversation was full of the turgid phrase and movement of melodrama. His presence anywhere was a constant sensation.

There was a strange mixture of treachery and generous good-fellowship in the expression of his face. When younger, before a long course of dissipation had left its marks upon him, he must have been very handsome. He was yet tall and tolerably erect, and the excessive measure of the liquor he had consumed showed itself, not so much in his face as in that peculiar bend to the knees, when walking, which the acute observer will always find the surest test of the confirmed Bacchanalian.

There is a kind of life that never gets into books, — a species of villany that floats ethereally just above the atmosphere of the courts. The newspaper reporter does not quite grasp it, and so it remains without its literature. Of a quarter-century or more of this indescribable sort of life Governor Dorr had skimmed the cream, as I may say.

All that was worldly he knew, from the infinitesimal series of negative physical pleasures to the most abstruse calculus of positive crime. The idea of a virtuous home, of children, and of scenes that are so common in every-day life was to him, I am sure, a memory of remote years. He saw all these things from the outside, and lived, even in his most lavish prosperity, in the very worst of homelessness. Yet I have seen him manifest simplicity as honest as a child's, and a tenderness in which there could be no counterfeit.

I think I have never known a man on whom a striking scene in nature had so powerful an effect. He would look upon a beautiful or wild landscape for hours at a time. There could have been no affectation in this, for he rarely expressed his admiration audibly ; and when he did, it was in some brief exclamation that was forcible or original.

I shall always remember the evening when we sat upon the quarter-deck of a steamboat at a backwoods landing, on one of the great Western rivers, where for some reason we were detained.

We were sitting alone, I think. It was nearly midnight, and there was scarcely a cloud in the heavens or a ripple in the water. The moon was shining grandly, duplicating in shadow the thick forests for miles along the stream. The Governor had been looking in silence at the magnificent scene for as much as a half-hour when I took occasion to remark that I thought I would go to my state-room.

The words were scarcely uttered when he startled me by jumping suddenly to his feet and exclaiming, his voice all a-quiver : " Great God ! a man does not see three such nights as this in a lifetime ; how can you — how can they sleep ? I shall not go to bed till the moon does !"

And as I left him, he sat down again with the determined yet injured look of one who had been insulted through nature.

The Governor liked to pass for a great literary character, and I believe he succeeded in his ambition among his peculiar associates. By a lucky chance I have found, between the leaves of an old diary which I kept spasmodically at that time, a specimen of his production. It is an elaborate " Life of Michael Mitchell, the Comedian and Dancer." I cut it out of a Cincinnati paper, — the Commercial, if I am not mistaken; and I am not sure that I did not once admire it almost as much as did the Governor himself.

I see now, by the light of greater technical knowledge in such matters, that this rare bit of biography was printed bodily as an advertisement. It has, after the manner of special patent-medicine notices, " Communicated " just over it, in brackets. I observe, too, that it has at the left-hand bottom corner these cabalistic signs : " d1t." I am glad, nevertheless, to be able to give an extract or so.

The opening sentence has, as will be seen, a striking though inadvertent allusion to one of the games with which the old gambler was doubt-less much more familiar than he could have been with the hazardous Latin. " The subject of this sketch," writes the biographer, "was born in Ireland, on the 20th of November, Anno Domino 1831."

A more extended extract, taken at random, — say from his account of Mitchell's first triumph, — will be all that is needed as a specimen of the Governor's average literary manner. It is better still, however, as an autobiographical reminiscence of the biographer himself, or, perhaps I should say, as a photograph of his own picturesque mind. You will observe how his style reeks of the drama and yellow-covered memories. That was the exact manner of his ordinary conversation.

It cannot be that he has weathered the years which have intervened since he made this contribution to literature; but it will always have this peculiarity for me, that I shall never read it without seeing the old adventurer, living and swaggering before me, the same insolvable riddle in human nature. Here is the paragraph : —

" We next find Mike in the difficult situation of vocalist and bone-player; he becomes a troubadour the 10th of March, 1842, a day sacred to men of genius (for on that day Tyrone Power, that excellent wit and comedian, left the shores of this country on the ill-fated President, never to return). On that identical day there was bustle and excitement in the castle of the Mitchells, No. 222 Greenwich Street, New York City. Young Michael was to be caparisoned and enter the lists 'armed cap-a-pie,' as a knight or troubadour of olden time (*vide* James). The

eventful eve of that eventful day arrived precisely
at nightfall, at the moment that 'Old Trinity'
proclaimed with brazen notes the hour of 7 P. M.
There issued from the outer gate of the Mitchells'
guarded palace a youth armed with four bones.
The night looked lowering as dark Fate itself, no
portents were in the sky, no Corsican Brothers illusions; but something made our hero tremble, —
it was the uncertainty of the future.   Sustaining
himself with a glass of root-beer, he made his way
through the obscurity of the gas-light to a dilap-
idated house, No. 450 Broadway, gave the counter-
sign or word of the night (Daniel Tucker, Esq.),
the door flew open at the magical sound, and
Michael entered.   At first sight of the interior of
that magnificent arena our hero's cheek slightly
paled, and well it might.   'The Chamber of Hor-
rors of Madame Tassarend' could not move the
redoubtable Michael now, for he has grown bold
in his profession.   But on that night, armed only
with youth and 'bones,' surrounded by a live
rattlesnake, a six-legged horse, three ladies in
wax, the counterpart of three of flesh that had
'shuffled off this mortal coil' by the hands of midnight murders [*sic*], — six little orphan boys armed

all with bones, and looking precious hungry, and
seated on six little chairs, a seventh chair vacant
for Mike himself, like that of Banquo's, — six junk-
bottles with six tallow-candles therein, throwing
their furtive, flickering, melancholy light upon
these cadaverous and superannuated 'Tarmon'
musicians,playing upon bass-drum,cracked fife,and
hurdy-gurdy. No wonder that poor Mike's blood
rushed to his heart, and that he trembled in his
boots ; the sight would have intimidated stronger
and older artists. The trio commenced their overture, — the music, that beautiful air, 'The Light
of Other Days' (poor fellows! the light of their
days had surely faded, — they were blind), and as
they proceeded with their soul-stirring drum and
ear-piercing fife, Mike recovered his self-posses-
sion. The martial music over, and the Germans
having retired to the shades of a lager-beer saloon,
Michael's turn came next. Taking the vacant
chair and seating himself thereon, he drew his
American castanets (the younger brother of the
banjo) from his pocket (he had but one at that
time), and threw himself in an attitude to *sustain*
himself for the coming fray ; it came at last, — the
rattle, the crash of seven juvenile bone-players in

8

the difficult overture to the opera of Daniel Tucker. It was awful, — it ended, and the applause shook the old tenement to its foundation."

Of Mitchell himself I can recollect little more than that he was a jovial, easy sort of fellow personally, and that he was, as his scenic biographer would have said, " a first-rate Ethiopian artist." Scandal had it that this same biographer, who was, it must be remembered, his business manager and partner, did risk the earnings of Mr. Mitchell's minstrels in hazardous back-rooms, and thus precipitated a catastrophe which the want of harmony among the members would sooner or later have brought upon the troupe.

In the absence of positive knowledge on the subject, I would not like to say how true or false this rumor was. This much only I will vouch for : we were advertised to perform in some city of Southern Ohio, and, going down to the depot with our big and little boxes, green-baize bags and fiddle-cases, we were startled with the announcement that there was no money in the treasury to pay our way out of Cincinnati.

I remember that the veteran German violinist,

scratching his wig, — which I need hardly say he had lived to recover, — and squeezing his violin under his arm, remarked, when he heard this piece of news, " Well, den de gombany ish bust!"

And, in point of fact, that veteran violinist was right.

I was afterward one of the volunteers at the grand complimentary benefit given to Mitchell at Cincinnati, with the proceeds of which he was sent out to California to join his friends Birch and Backus.

Mitchell, poor fellow, like Lynch and Sliter and so many of my old associates in the cork-opera, has passed away, let us hope to a quieter stage, beyond the double-dealing of managers and the contumely of publicans.

An old showman is, in truth, a being *sui gene-ris.* You rarely meet one who will not tell you he has been twenty-two years in the show business. He always talks in hyperbole, uses adjectives for adverbs, and arranges all the minor incidents of his life, as well as his conversation, in the most dramatic forms. He is often a better friend to others than to himself; he is not naturally worse than the majority of men, but has more temptation. A good negro-minstrel would, in any other profession, be an Admirable Crichton in respect to morals.

While acknowledging with pride that I met in this calling some who deserved even such praise, it is due to the truth to state also that I have known many and many a poor fellow who was, in the language of Addison, —

> "Reduced, like Hannibal, to seek relief
> From court to court, and wander up and down,
> A vagabond in Afric."

CHAPTER VII.

ON THE FLOATING PALACE.

THE day after the farewell benefit of Mitchell I was engaged by Dr. Spaulding, the veteran manager, whose old quarrel with Dan Rice has made him famous to the lovers of the circus. He was then fitting out the Floating Palace for its voyage on the Western and Southern rivers.

The Floating Palace was a great boat built expressly for show purposes. It was towed from place to place by a steamer called the James Raymond. The Palace contained a museum with all the usual concomitants of "Invisible Ladies," stuffed giraffes, puppet-dancing, &c., &c. The Raymond contained, besides the dining-hall and state-rooms of the employees, a concert-saloon fitted up with great elegance and convenience, and called the "Ridotto." In this latter I was engaged, in conjunction with "a full band of minstrels," to do my jig and wench dances.

The two boats left Cincinnati with nearly a hundred souls on board, that being the necessary complement of the vast establishment. We were bound for Pittsburg, where we were to give our first exhibition ; purposing to stop afterward, on our way down, at all the towns and landings along the Ohio. Everything went well on our way up the river till we came within about twenty miles of Wheeling, Va., when the Raymond stuck fast on a sand-bar.

It was thought best for the people to be transferred to the Palace, so as to lighten the steamer and let her work off. When, accordingly, we had all huddled into the museum, our lines were cast off and our anchor let go ; but we were carried half a mile down stream before the anchor caught. Here, all day, from the decks of the Palace we could watch the futile efforts of the Raymond to get off the bar. The only provision for the inner man, on board of our craft, was a drinking-saloon, which was of very little comfort to the numerous ladies of the party, to say the least. Toward night we became exceedingly hungry, but no relief was sent us from the steamer.

One Riesse, an obese bass-singer, who was a

terrible gourmand, and who had been for the last five hours raving about the decks in a pitiable manner, rushed suddenly out upon the guard, about eight o'clock, declaring that he saw a boat-load of provisions coming from the Raymond. A shout of joy now went up from the famished people that shook the stuffed giraffes and wax-works in their glass cases.

It was a boat, indeed ; but it contained simply the captain, mate, and pilot, who had come all that way after their evening bitters at the drink-ing-saloon. They expressed themselves very sorry for us, and were confident that they could now get the steamer off the bar. This liquid stimulus was all that had been needed from the first.

With this mild assurance for a foundation to our hopes of relief, they took their departure, and we waited on and on through the long night. Riesse, the bass-singer, never slept a wink, or allowed many others to sleep ; his hungry voice, like a loon's on some solitary lake, breaking in upon the stillness where and when it was least expected. Wrapped in the veritable cloak of the great Pacha Mohammed Ali, I drowsed through

the latter part of the night, crouched down between the glass apartments of the waxen Tam
O'Shanter and the Twelve Apostles.

In the morning there were several more steamers aground in the neighborhood, but no better
prospect of the Raymond's getting clear. We
were finally taken off to her in small boats, and
allowed to break our long fast.

Instead of rising, the river fell, and we were left
almost a week on dry land. Our provisions giving out, it was thought best for the performers to
be taken up to Wheeling by a little stern-wheeler
that happened to come along. At that city we
gave several exhibitions in Washington Hall.
Proceeding thence down the river, on the stern-
wheeler, to play at the towns along till we should
be overtaken by the Palace and the Raymond, we
passed those unfortunate boats, still laboring to
free themselves, and were greeted with hearty
cheers by the people on board. One night the
river rose suddenly, and in a day or so we were
overtaken by the whole establishment, at Marietta,
Ohio.

The purposed trip to Pittsburg was abandoned.
We commenced our voyage down the river, ex-

hibiting in the afternoon and evening, and sometimes in the morning, at two, and often three towns or landings in a day.

It needed not this excess of its labors to tire me of the showman's life. Several months before I had begun to doubt whether a great negro-minstrel was a more enviable man than a great senator or author. As these doubts grew on me, I purchased some school-books, and betook myself to study every day, devouring, in the intervals of arithmetic and grammar, the contents of every work of biography and poetry that I could lay hands on.

The novelty and excitement of this odd life, indeed, were wearing away. All audiences at last looked alike to me, as all lecture-goers do to Dr. Holmes. They laughed at the same places in the performance, applauded at the same place, and looked inane or interested at the same place, day after day, week after week, and month after month.

I became gradually indifferent to their applause, or only noticed when it failed at the usual step or pantomime. Then succeeded a sort of contempt for audiences, and, at last, a positive hatred of them and myself. I noticed, or thought I noticed, that their faces wore the same vacant expression whether their eyes were staring at me or the stuffed giraffes or the dancing puppets of the museum.

Nevertheless the days, and nights too, on the Palace were eventful ones. Some unexpected thing was always happening to the boats, or to the performers, or to the audiences. An occasional struggle with the town authorities would add spice to our life. What made these squabbles particularly interesting was that they never resulted twice alike. The one that caused us the most merriment, and, consequently, dwells best in my memory, occurred on the Ohio, at West Columbia, Va.

Certain authorities at that ambitious little town had agreed with our agent that our license should be the sum of two dollars and fifty cents, which was merely reasonable in those days, so innocent of our later improvements in taxation. But when we had opened our doors to the vast multitude on the banks, certain others of the authorities became suddenly impressed with the idea that the agreement with the agent was based on too cheap a plan, and demanded twenty-five dollars or the shows could not go on.

Our manager strenuously refused, but offered at last to compromise rather than have any further trouble, tendering twelve dollars and a half. The authorities persisted in their unreasonable demand, and said, with still greater flourish of constables, &c. that the shows should not go on.

It was the work of about ten minutes to cast off the lines and float down stream a few rods, just outside the limits of the corporation ; and the shows did go on, without paying any license at all, and to overflowing and sympathizing audiences.

Shortly after, at another little town in Kentucky, a runaway couple came into the museum, bringing the squire with them ; and right in front of the glass case where a stuffed hyena and a hilarious alligator, also stuffed, exchanged perpetual smiles at each other, — which, of course, were intended by the taxidermist as looks of ferocity, — and while a barrel-organ was playing a lively dance for the puppets, this runaway young couple was married.

A brother of the lady arrived on the scene just

too late to prevent the nuptials. The only means
of revenge he could think of was to get abominably drunk, and raise a disturbance in the concert-room that afternoon. It must have been a
memorable day with that particular family, for the
young gentleman was roundly whipped for his
share in the wedding ceremonies.

The row, however, became general. That was
the momentous occasion when Governor Dorr,
entering the arena by a side door, announced
with some emphasis that he wanted it understood
he had something to say in that fight. He was
standing on a seat by the door when he commenced this speech. It was never ended, at least
to his satisfaction. He had just begun his exor-
dium as reported, when some stalwart Kentuck-
ian knocked him clear through the door.

With remarkable presence of mind the Governor picked up his hat as if he had merely happened to drop it on the guard of the boat, and
walked quietly off to his state-room, leaving the
regular ushers to restore order.

If I have not before mentioned Dorr's presence on the Palace, it has been because I have
been trying to explain in my puzzled memory how

he came there, and what was the line of his duties. I should have put him down at once as the literary gentleman of the establishment, were it not for the fact that we had another who manifestly filled that office.

I allude to the gentleman who edited the daily paper which was printed in the museum and distributed gratuitously to its patrons. This man was the founder and for a long time the editor of one of the best-known and most influential journals now published in the Union. The wreck of a fine scholar and a graphic writer, who had been the associate of some of the highest and best of our land, it was a melancholy sight to see him industriously printing his little paper before the stolid, curious people who thronged about his stand.

At the same stand gingerbread and brilliant-colored candies and lemonade were dispensed, — pale red lemonade, which seemed, as one might say, continually beholding its maker, and only half succeeding in its attempt to blush. Poor old fellow! the labor of his hands and brain was, as I have remarked, distributed gratuitously. The lemonade was sold for five cents a glass.

This thought, if it ever occurred to him, could have had little force, for his philosophy taught him to accept every situation unmurmuringly. He had but one argument to establish his theory of fate, and he was never weary of repeating it. When any passing philanthropist would grapple with him and endeavor to show him that he ought to be very miserable, he would tell this story.

"There was a man," he would say, "at work on a scaffold of a four-story building in Cincinnati. The scaffolding gave way, and he fell those four stories, and one besides, down into the cellar. Fifteen minutes thereafter he was up again, uninjured, at his work. A week afterward he was walking in front of Alf Burnett's saloon, stepped on a watermelon-rind, fell, broke his neck, and died instantly."

The narrator would never vouchsafe any explanation. When his hearer, making an application for himself, would accuse our philosopher of fatalism, he would only smile good-naturedly, and go about his duties. It must, indeed, have been a dull penetration that could see nothing better in the old fellow's story, — especially under the every-day commentary of his uncomplaining life. And I am glad to say others put this larger interpretation upon him and his philosophy, that his own misfortunes had taught him, more than his story, the ways of God are inscrutable; that He is all in all, and that, high or low, successful or broken, we are all alike in His merciful hands.

Scarcely three years ago I saw my old friend for the last time. We met in the street at San Francisco, where he then lived, and where he has since died. How well he was known and loved there was in some measure attested by the honorable manner of his burial.

There are few printers, at least, in the metropolis of the Pacific who will not remember him, although they may have known nothing more of his personal history than that he was the veteran *attaché* of Calhoun's job-rooms. Whatever the straits to which his peculiar misfortune brought him, he never lost that indescribable dignity and courtesy which were a part of his heritage as a born gentleman.

Poor old John McCreary! he would have written a better obituary of me than this, and published it in his Palace Journal, if I had chanced to get knocked on the head in some of the riots and perilous fights which we witnessed together at those lawless backwoods landings.

And this brings me back again to Governor Dorr, who was sore in the face, and more especially in the feelings, for some time after his disastrous attempt to reason with the excited spirits of that Kentucky audience. He could not bear, with any degree of equanimity, the slightest allusion to the day of the marriage in the museum.

I cannot remember exactly when the Governor left the Palace, or why he was, as I have already intimated, ever one of the company. I lean to the opinion that the manager, or his right-hand man, the once famous Van Orden of Dan Rice's satirical song, kept him on board to be amused by his conversation.

Except this amusing conversation, and a commendable regularity at meals, I can think of no activity whatever on the part of the Governor while with us, — save only that he did two things: the first was to get knocked through the door of the concert-room, as before mentioned; and the second was to write up for our daily newspaper, the Palace Journal, a most brilliant account of the curiosities in the museum.

The picturesque joy with which, in that series of articles, he would pursue the history of some bogus war-club through the hands and over the heads of whole dynasties of savage kings; the sunny sea voyages upon which he would send his adventurous rhetoric to far tropic islands after some insignificant shell, which, perhaps, was in reality captured in the neighborhood of Long Branch; the fearful and bloody deeds of midnight assassins that he would group about some old rusty sheaf-knife, which was curious only because it had been rusted to order by chemicals; and then the melting tenderness in which his soul would go out in the heart history of our wax figures, — especially of that stolid, blue-eyed lady in excessive black lashes and pink cheeks, who had been bought with an odd lot from an old collection at Albany, and attired in cheap gauze and labelled "The Empress Josephine," — these delightful arabesques of invention and sentiment, and, in a word, any of the Governor's fine literary pyrotechnics may not be reproduced.

They have gone down with the last files of the

Palace Journal, who shall say in what Western Lethe? And yet I have the bad taste to own that, for my own reading, I would rather come across that series of descriptive articles now than upon the lost books of Livy.

The Governor fairly revelled in his work. Indeed, my last memory of him is as I saw him, with his lead-pencil in his hand and indefinite foolscap before him, sprawled out upon his stomach on the floor of the museum, one forenoon when there was no exhibition. He was staring, in a fine frenzy, straight into the distended mouth and merry glass eyes of our stuffed alligator; in the act, no doubt, was the ecstatic Governor of inventing and composing details of the heart-rending tragedy of the last man swallowed by the smiling, convivial saurian before him.

And there I shall leave him.

CHAPTER VIII.

WILD LIFE.

I OBTAINED my first view of the great
Mississippi and of the practical working of
Lynch law at the same time. The night of our
advent at Cairo was lit up by the fires of an
execution.

A negro, it seems, was the owner or lessee of
an old wharf-boat, which had been moored to the
levee of that town, and which he had turned to
the uses of a gambling-saloon. People who had
been enticed into it had never been seen or heard
of afterward. The vigilance committee, then gov-
erning Cairo, had frequently endeavored to lay
hold of the negro and bring him to trial ; but he
had secret passages from one part of the wharf-
boat to the other, by which he always eluded his
pursuers.

Having no doubt that he was guilty of several
murders, the *vigilantes*, on the night of our ar-

rival, had come down to the levee, two or three hundred strong, armed, equipped, and determined to make the wretch surrender. In answer to their summons they received nothing but insults from the negro, still out of sight and secure in one of his hiding-places.

At a given signal the wharf-boat was set on fire and cut adrift, and as it floated out into the current the *vigilantes* surrounded it in small boats, with their rifles ready and pointed to prevent the escape of their victim.

When the wharf-boat was well into the stream the negro appeared boldly at the place which, in the middle of all river-craft of that kind, is left open for the reception and discharge of freight. And now a scene occurred, so sensationally dramatic, so easily adaptable to the stage of these latter days, that I would not dare to relate it for truth if I had not witnessed it with my own eyes.

The negro was not discovered till he had rolled a large keg of powder into the middle of the open space just mentioned. As he stood in the light of his burning craft, it could be seen by the people in the small boats in the river that he had a cocked musket with the muzzle plunged into the keg of powder. Then the negro dared them to come on and take him, pouring upon them at the same time such horrible oaths and curses as have rarely come from the lips of man.

The small boats kept a proper distance now, their occupants caring only to prevent his escape into the water. As the flames grew thicker around him there the negro stood, floating down into the darkness that enveloped the majestic river, with his cocked musket still in the keg of powder, and cursing and defying his executioners. He was game to the last. We heard the explosion down the stream, and saw the wharf-boat sink.

The next day I spoke with the leader of the band in the small boats, — a short, wiry little man, with a piercing eye. He said that he had not the heart to shoot the "nigger," because he showed such pluck. He even confessed that, for the same reason, he felt almost sorry for the victim, after the explosion had blown him into eternity.

We saw, indeed, a great deal of wild life in the country we visited, for we steamed thousands of

miles on the Western and Southern rivers. We
went, for instance, the entire navigable lengths
of the Cumberland and Tennessee. Our adver-
tising agent had a little boat of his own, in which
he preceded us. The Palace and Raymond would
sometimes run their noses upon the banks of
some of these rivers where there was not a hab-
itation in view, and by the hour of the exhibition the boats and shore would be thronged
with people. In some places on the Mississippi,
especially in Arkansas, men would come in with
pistols sticking out of their coat-pockets, or with
long bowie-knives protruding from the legs of
their boots.

The manager had provided for these savage
people ; for every member of the company was
armed, and, at a given signal, stood on the defensive. We had a giant for a doorkeeper, who
was known in one evening to kick down stairs as
many as five of these bushwhackers, with drawn
knives in their hands. There were two other
persons, employed ostensibly as ushers, but really
to fight the wild men of the rivers. These two
gentlemen were members of the New York prize
ring, — one of whom, I believe, went to England

with Heenan at the time of the international "mill," and whose name I saw in a New York paper, the other day, as the trainer of a pugilistic celebrity of the present time.

The honest fellows scorned to use anything but their fists in preserving order; and it is strange, considering the number of deadly weapons drawn on them, that they never received anything worse than a few scratches. Nor did they, indeed, ever leave their antagonists with anything worse than a broken head; except in a solitary case, which befell at a backwoods landing on the Upper Mississippi, where a person who had made an unprovoked attack on the boats was left for dead upon the bank, as we pushed out into the stream. We never heard whether he lived or died.

Besides these pugilists, we had in our company other celebrities; for instance, the amiable and gentlemanly David Reed, whose character-song of "Sally come up" made such a *furore*, not long ago, in New York, and, I believe, throughout the country. His picture is to be seen at all the music-stores.

One other of our company has since had his name and exploits telegraphed to the remotest ends of the earth ; I remember to have read of him myself, in a little German newspaper, on the banks of the Danube. This was Professor Lowe, the balloonist, late of the Army of the Potomac. I doubt much whether the Professor had dipped very deeply into aeronautics at that time. He was an ingenious, odd sort of Yankee, with his long hair braided and hanging in two tails down his back.

His wife, formerly a Paris *danseuse*, was my instructor in the Terpsichorean art. By the aid of a little whip, which she insisted was essential to success, she taught me to go through all the posturings and pirouettes of the operatic ballet-girls. I was forced often to remonstrate against the ardor with which she applied her whip to a toe or finger of mine that would get perversely out of the line of beauty.

Professor Lowe and Madame, his wife, conducted the performances of the " Invisible Lady," a contrivance that may not be familiar to all my readers. A hollow brass ball with four trumpets protruding from it is suspended inside of a hollow railing. Questions put by the by-standers are answered through a tube by a person in the apart-

ment beneath. The imaginations of the spectators make the sounds seem to issue from the brass
ball. It used to be amusing to stand by and listen
to the answers of the " Invisible Lady," *alias*
Madame Lowe, whose English was drolly mixed
up with her own vernacular. But if the responses
were sometimes unintelligible, this only added to
the mystery and success of the brazen oracle.

The Professor was passionately fond of game.
He was struck with the abundance of turkeys in
one of the Southern States where we chanced to
be, and, throwing his gun across his shoulder,
sallied forth to bring some of them down. He
returned shortly with two large black birds, which
he exhibited about the decks, amid the grins and
suppressed laughter of the crew. It was not till
the Professor took his game into the kitchen to
have it dressed for dinner that he was informed,
not only that his birds were not turkeys at all,
but that he had been breaking one of the statutes
of the State, which prohibits, under a pecuniary
penalty, the killing of turkey-buzzards.

The Professor had a young bear which he
bought for twenty dollars at some one of our
stopping-places. Now this was the most mis-

chievous cub that I ever happened to see. To
say nothing of the number of stuffed snakes and
pelicans which he devoured or tore to pieces,
the degree of havoc he could make in a trunk
of wigs and stage wardrobe was something just
simply astounding. I have known him to eat up,
or at least cause to vanish, in the space of a
single riotous hour, all that was necessary to the
artistic " make-up " of three old men, a half-dozen
plantation darkies, and I know not how many
Shaker women. That was the time when he
plundered a large property-box.

That bear was chained and whipped, and made
sick by the necessary poisons of taxidermy, but he
bore all with perfect cheerfulness. Three days
after a contest with a stuffed animal he was always more playful than ever.

There was something very ludicrous in the
good-natured leer he put on when the Professor
was experimenting upon some new way of confin-
ing him. As soon as the people were well asleep,
if the bear chanced to have any curiosity about
the contents of a lady's bandbox in some remote
state-room, or about the quality of the pantryman's
supply of sugar, he was always sure to break loose,

and confiscate on his return any odd pair of pantaloons or boots that a sleeper had unconsciously exposed before retiring. Thus it happened that young Bruin had his enemies.

He had his friends, too, and I was one of them. For there was something very lovable about that bear, after all : he was so rollicking, and his black hide, from the burnished peak of his jolly nose to the end of the stub of his syncopated tail, did so seem to gleam in the light of hearty good-fellowship!

He was especially irresistible when any one took notice of him in his penal exile, away off in the dim region of the gas-machine. Then he would lie over on his young back and invite his friend to a romp, in a manner that showed hospitality in every movement of his chubby paws. Or if in the mood to receive his visitor open-armed, he would rise courteously on his hind feet, his tongue hanging lackadaisically out of one side of his mouth, and his roguish eyes assisting the smile which spread from ear to ear ; and he would, in short, look as amiably foolish and sheepish as people are said to look who are about to indulge in a hug.

If his chain interfered with him at these receptions — and it often did — he would turn his droll
orbs askant upon it, apparently in the same sort
of playful humor that human prisoners so often
indulge in at the expense and to the ridicule of
their bolts and bars.   Indeed, the young rascal
always carried a human sympathy with him.

By his admirers, at least, some ameliorating
circumstance was sure to be found in all his most
daring and damaging exploits.   There were some,
I believe, who tried to excuse even what I shall
now have to mention as the crowning atrocity of
his life.

The plea of his apologists was his manifest freedom from any shade of theological bias, as proved
by the calmly ludicrous deliberation of the deed
itself.   I will not express an opinion, although
there is not the least doubt in my mind that the
doors of the wax-work cases should have been
more securely fastened.   I will merely say that
there *was* something very grave and candid withal in his manner, when caught in the very act of
scalping one of the Twelve Apostles.

This feat aroused his enemies to the highest
pitch of indignation, and they clamored for ven-

geance on Professor Lowe's bear. The cub's friends, however, did not desert him in the hour of his evil report. And so, at last, a Guelph and Ghibelline division ran through the whole company.

The manager, treasurer, cook, pantryman, such gentlemen as had been left to make their breakfast toilets without boots or other more necessary articles of apparel, and all the ladies even to Madame Lowe herself, were of the anti-bear party.

All the performers, except those who had been ravished of wigs and tights or other miscellaneous pieces of wardrobe, the engineer of the gas-machine which furnished light for the whole establishment, all the prize-fighters, and, in a word, all the reckless characters of the two boats, headed by the determined Professor himself, marched, as I may say, figuratively, under the banner of the bear.

The factions were about equally divided, and equally impressed with the merit of their respective causes. We of the bear party, however, had one manifest advantage. The captain of the boats, jolly old William McCracken — as fat as he was jolly, and as honest as he was fat — was on our side.

Such a state of feeling could not, as may be well imagined, exist for any long time among so many people, and in the narrow limits of those two boats, without some act of aggression from one side or the other.   And it came.

One of the prize-fighters, perhaps in simple defiance to the opposition, and perhaps in a burst of honest sympathy with the cub himself— I cannot say which, for he was of my party — purloined from the dressing-room and presented to young Bruin, in his durance, a pair of cast-off pantaloons in which a certain minstrel was in the habit of performing his great act of the " comb solo."

Of course, the actor was indignant ; and, whether in bodily fear of the prize-fighter, or believing what he said, maintained that the infernal bear had been loose again, and vowed that he would have his life.   The act of the prize-fighter was certainly ill-advised and hazardous, not merely to the pantaloons, but to the bear himself.   I mention it as only one more instance of the danger in which one stands from his own friends, especially if he chance to be at all prominent in times of great partisan strife.

The cub's enemies now clamored more loudly

than ever against him, stoutly asserting that
chains and gas-rooms were not strong enough to
hold him; and the ladies were still more sure that
he would bite. One young mother, I remember,
related that she had heard of a well-authenticated
instance wherein a single bear, I think she said,
had come out of the woods and massacred and
devoured forty children.

In the middle of the night after the presenta-
tion of the pantaloons, a disguised band, headed,
it was afterwards supposed, by the comb-soloist
himself, stealthily gained the prison of the bear,
broke his chain, and threw him overboard. The
next morning triumph was in the faces of the
opposition, and surprise and grief in the hearts
of Professor Lowe and his liegemen.

Of course, no one knew how or when the bear
had disappeared. Gradually the grins of the anti-
bears widened into laughter; then they spoke to
one another for our benefit, in those peculiar gib-
ing tones which may be called audible grins; then
their asides became soliloquy, and finally straight
dialogue addressed by victorious Montagues to
aggrieved Capulets. Our side manifestly having
the worst of it, our feeble retorts were soon

drowned in the *Io Triumphe* torrent of our enemies and the bear's.

At last, when the exulting taunts of the opposition were at their height, the Professor discovered his bear, sitting very quietly and philosophically on the rudder of the Palace, to which he had swum and up which he had clambered, when thrown into the river in the night. A boat was sent after him straightway; and, for a time, the thunderstruck anti-bear party were crushed. Bruin's receptions that day were more popular with his friends, if possible, than they had ever been before. He was more than a hero, now; he was a martyr.

A ponderous padlock was found and placed upon the door of the gas-room, and the real leader of our party was considered safe. Yet there was something ominously silent about the opposition for the next week. They made very few threats, but there was plainly murder in their thoughts. I make, of course, no account of those ignoble attempts of his foes to prove that the cub, notwithstanding our defensive vigilance, had once more got into the cases.

These tentative frauds defeated themselves

from the very wantonness in which they were conceived. It was out of all reason to suppose that a bear would have placed the hat of the inebriate Tam O'Shanter upon the head of the noble Helen Mar ; and it was still more out of reason and unnatural to think him guilty of so arranging the waxen "father of his country," George Washington, that he should be discovered the next morning astride the stuffed alligator, in the exact plight of that famous traveller, Mr. Waterton.

These things were, in truth, too preposterous to be entertained for a moment. If the Lady Helen had been robbed of her back hair, it was argued, or if the hilarious reptile had been rent limb from limb, or the meditative George Washington had been jerked out of his top-boots and left prostrate in his case, with bald head and torn garments, there would have been a smack of probability and of ursine humor and prowess in the deeds.

No, — there was something too absurd and human about these frauds ; and it was a minor triumph for us when they were traced shortly afterward, by the irate manager, to a party of

5 *

late wassailers in the drinking-saloon of the museum.

I suppose we grew careless in our manifest ascendency, for one morning at a landing in a wild, thick-wooded country a hunter came on board with bear-meat to sell, and, by a strange fatality, almost the first man he accosted as a probable purchaser was Professor Lowe himself. This reminded the great aeronaut of his own animal, which he had not yet visited that morning. While the Professor was absent at the gas-room one of the opposition came up and purchased what the hunter had to sell, and bore it to the kitchen, — exchanging, by the by, very significant glances with those of his party he met on the way.

In a moment more the Professor was back, in earnest conversation with the hunter, and it spread like wildfire over the two boats that the cub was gone for good this time, — or, rather, that he was cooking for dinner. The hunter told his honest story, of how he had been awakened by his dogs in the middle of the night, and had pursued and shot the bear. There were a dozen different traces going to show that the prisoner of the gas-room had been released by human hands, and pursued on the shore with sticks and clubs.

It never transpired exactly who were the perpetrators of the foul deed. Our party, I need scarcely add, were utterly nonplussed and demoralized, while the opposition were correspondingly elate. And these latter, bent upon the additional cannibalism of devouring their arch enemy, had him served up at table before our face and eyes.

But when each of our party had scornfully refused to partake of our deceased friend, and when the plates of the opposition were helped bountifully, even to those of the ladies, — to whose credit be it said, that they turned their faces while they passed their plates, — a partisan of the late cub arose from his seat and made a few remarks. In a quiet but forcibly specific way, he called the attention of the banqueters to the amount of stuffed specimens they were about to entertain with their bear-meat, and ended by congratulating them upon the intimate knowledge of taxidermy and natural history which would likely be the result.

I think I never knew a speech to make so

powerful an effect. The opposition party, almost to a man, and certainly to each individual woman, left the table; the remains of the unfortunate bear were removed, and tenderly consigned to the river; and his faithful friends ate their dinners in a final triumph that was half assured and all melancholy.

CHAPTER IX.

IN his social relations a performer, like many another great man or woman, is liable to mistakes of head and heart. It is a pretty generally known fact, for instance, that the most famous tenor of our day is so careful of his gloves as to fly into a towering rage with any lady who touches them with more than her finger-tips, in the most impassioned duets. And a very celebrated *prima donna* who takes the world captive as much by the exceeding loveliness of her person and manner as by her wonderful voice, is in the habit of beating her maid abominably two or three times a week.

It would, indeed, be an acute analysis which should determine just what it is in the higher walks of music that makes the lives of its special votaries so strikingly inharmonious. He or she who has known of an operatic company wherein

the four leading persons were on speaking terms
with one another, off the stage, has known a
remarkable fact in the history of that peculiar
class.

Of these, and of the dramatic profession proper,
I would perhaps have no right to speak here,
were it not for the fact that, in my time at least,
there was a sort of fraternity among all people
who appeared before foot-lights. I do not know
whether the members of cork-opera associate with
the better class of actors at this day ; but I think
they do not. I would venture to assert, however,
that among the lower orders of actors, minstrels,
and circus-riders there ever will be such a spirit
of bohemianism — such a touch of hearty, reckless good-nature — as will always make their
whole world kin.

Indeed, an honest old professional friend of
mine, whom I met last winter, spoke of lecturing
as " the show-business." There may have been
more or less of truth in his remark. This, at least,
is no time or place to discuss the question. But
there was, indubitably, in this extending of the
right hand of fellowship from the side show to the
lyceum, a fine illustration of the catholic spirit
which links the " profession " together.

Jealousy may be set down as the chief failing of the whole race, high or low. I have known men, whose names have made some noise in the world, to measure with straws the comparative sizes of the letters in which they were announced on a poster. But among minstrels, especially, a thorough wordliness and boon-companionship enable them generally to be civil to one another, whatsoever their private feelings.

An old showman, at last, comes to look upon the quiet ways of ordinary life with that same kind of longing, romantic interest with which a certain species of imaginative youth are always looking upon the impossible glory of travelling with a show. A droll sighing for rural pursuits seems to be the most common form taken by the romance of your veteran itinerant. Yet, oddly enough, there is scarcely any one whom he holds, personally, in such ridiculous contempt as he does the honest farmer.

The vow which the old sailor in the forecastle is forever making to go to sea no more, is rarely remembered over three days on land. And so it is with the cognate ideal which floats in the queer imagination of the old showman. I never knew but three or four who attained anything like the realization of their romantic purpose. Daniel Emmet — the author, I believe, of " Old Dan Tucker," " Jordan," and many of the best known of the earlier negro-melodies — did, toward the close of his life, so far reach the fleeting object of his bucolic ambition as to have a large, well-filled chicken-coop in the back yard of a rented house, in the suburbs of a great city.

This sentimental regard for nature was vented by the members of the first companies with which I travelled in fishing and camping parties along the borders of the inland lakes. They would swallow most execrable amateur cooking during the day, but a night with beetles and mosquitoes would, as a general thing, drive them back willing captives into the arms of effete civilization.

On the Floating Palace, Nature seemed to have taken us so closely to her bosom, in the wild lapse of those majestic rivers, that the romantic instinct of the oldest showman expressed itself oftenest in lazy expeditions to trap mocking-birds, or in listlessly dropping a line into the stream for cat-fish and soft-shelled turtles.

The ladies of the profession are sometimes given to gossip and backbiting in as great a degree at least as are the gentlemen. Jealousy may be as rife on a Mississippi show-boat as in the antechamber of any court in Europe. I have known a *danseuse* to furnish boys with clandestine bouquets to throw on the stage when she appeared; not that she cared at all for the praise or blame of the audience, but that she *did* care to crush a cleverer rival.

In our company on board the Palace and the Raymond we had strange contrasts in human nature. It would happen, for instance, that the man who could not sleep without snoring would be placed in the same state-room with the man who could not sleep within hearing of the most distant snore. The man who could not eat pork was seated at table just opposite the man who doted on it. We had one gentleman — the fleshy bass-singer already mentioned — who spent all his leisure in catching mocking-birds; and another, who passed his spare hours in contriving new and undiscoverable ways of letting these birds escape from the cages.

There were on board ladies who had seen more

prosperous days, when they were the chief attrac-
tions at the theatres of London, Paris, and New
York, — according to their own stories ; other
ladies who had never associated with such vulgar
people before ; other ladies who hoped they would
die if they did not leave the company at the very
next landing, but never left ; and yet other ladies,
I am rejoiced to add, who were lovely in nature
and deed, — kind mothers and faithful wives,
whose strength of character and ready cheerfulness tended as far as possible to restore the social
equilibrium.

In the course of the long association grotesque
friendships sprang up. The man who played the
bass-drum was the bosom companion of the man
who had charge of the machine for making the
gas which supplied the two boats. The pretty
man of the establishment, he who played the
chimes on the top of the museum and the piano
in the concert-room, — at present, a popular com-
poser at St. Louis, — this young gentleman, who
broke all the hearts of the country girls that came
into the show, was the inseparable friend of the
pilot, — a great, gruff, warm-hearted fellow, who
steered the Raymond from the corners of his eyes

and swore terribly at snags. The man who dusted down Tam O'Shanter and the Twelve Apostles in wax, and had especial care of the stuffed birds, giraffes, and alligators, was on most intimate terms with the cook.

The youngest of the ladies who hoped to die if they did n't go ashore at the next landing and never went, — or died either, for that matter,— well, she was, or pretended to be, desperately in love with the treasurer of the company, a thin, irascible old fellow with a bald head. On the arrival of another *danseuse* in the company, the two dancers, who were before deadly enemies, became sworn friends and confidantes, united in their jealousy and hatred of the new-comer. The lady who was loudest in proclaiming that she had never before associated with such low people as the performers on board of these boats seemed to enjoy herself most, and indeed spent most of her time in the society of Bridget, the Irish laundry-woman of the establishment, who on one occasion, after excessive stimulus, came very near hanging herself overboard to dry, instead of a calico dress.

As a general thing, however, the ladies, performers, and crew of our boats were not so quar-

relsome as I have seen a set of cabin passengers
on a sea voyage between America and Europe, or
especially on the three weeks' passage to or from
California.   When I consider that there were so
many of us together in this narrow compass for
nearly a year, it seems to me strange indeed that
there was not more bad blood excited.

Madame Olinza was, I believe, the name of the
Polish lady who walked on a tight-rope from the
floor of one end of the museum up to the roof of the
farthest gallery.   This kind of perilous ascension
and suspension was something new in the country then.   It was before the time of Blondin, and
Madame used to produce a great sensation.

Now it may be interesting to the general
reader to learn that this tight-rope walker was
one of the most exemplary, domestic little bodies
imaginable.   She and her husband had a large
state-room on the upper deck of the Raymond,
and she was always there with her child when
released from her public duties.

One afternoon the nurse happened to bring the
child into the museum when Madame Olinza was
on the rope ; and out of the vast audience that

little face was recognized by the fond mother, and her attention so distracted that she lost her balance, dropped her pole, and fell.

Catching the rope with her hands, however, in time to break her fall, she escaped fortunately without the least injury ; but ever after that her child was kept out of the audience while she was on the rope.

CHAPTER X.

GOING up the Mississippi from Cairo, we passed, one Sunday, the old French town of Cape Girardeau, Missouri, and its Roman Catholic college on the river-bank. The boys were out on the lawn under the trees, and I became as envious of their lot as I ever had been before of a man who worked on a steamboat or who danced "in the minstrels." I suddenly resolved that I would go to that college.

We did not stop at Cape Girardeau till our return down the river, some weeks afterward. Then I went boldly up, and sought an interview with the president of the institution. I found him to be a kindly-mannered priest, who encouraged me in my ambition. He told me it would be well to save up more money than I then had, and that he would do all he could for me. I returned to the Palace, and immediately gave warning that I purposed to leave as soon as some one could be got to fill my place.

It struck me as somewhat odd that it was six months from that date before I could get away. It has been explained to me since. The fact is, I received what, as a boy, I thought a good salary, but nothing like what I earned. It took two men afterwards to fill my place. I have been told since, that more than a year before that time, and prior to this last engagement, the late E. P. Christy had written for me from New York, but that the letter had been intercepted by those whose interest it then was that I should not know my own value in the "profession."

I used to see that my name was larger than almost any other on the bills, but was led to believe that it was because I was a boy, and not likely to excite the jealousy of the other members of the company. It may not be very soothing to my vanity, but, dwelling upon these things dispassionately, I have my honest doubts now whether I was not always a greater success as an advertisement than as a performer.

I was promised at New Orleans that, if I would go over to Galveston, Texas, with the minstrel troupe, I should certainly be allowed to retire from public life. So we left the Palace and the Raymond at the levee of the former city, and took passage in the regular steamship, crossing the Gulf to Galveston. We performed there two or three weeks with great success. Few minstrels then had wandered that way, and thus it happened that my farewell appearance as a dancer was greeted with a crowded house. Except as a poor lecturer, I have never been on the stage since I left Galveston.

Still resolved to go to college at Cape Girardeau, I returned to New Orleans, and took passage to Cairo on the steamer L. M. Kennett. Barney Williams and his wife were on board during the tedious voyage; but I suppose they have long since forgotten all about the urchin who surprised and bored them with his minute knowledge of the early history of the country through which we passed.

The river above Cairo, very much to my sorrow, was frozen over, for it was midwinter. There was no alternative for me but to proceed to Cape Girardeau by land, — a long, difficult, and expensive journey in those times. After a great deal of trouble and some danger, I arrived at the gates of the College, and proceeded directly to the room of the president.

The kindly face that I remembered so well again beamed upon me, as I stood before him and said that I had come to stay a year, at least, at his school. At his good-natured question as to how much money I had, I emptied my pocket of just thirty-five dollars in gold. That was the sum to which the unforeseen expenses of my long journey had reduced me.

The president, being aware that the river was frozen, — so that I could not get away even if I had had money enough to go with, — and having much greater discretionary power than the presidents of our Protestant colleges, told me that I might stay.

At the end of my year the river was again frozen, and the good president was again prevailed upon to keep me till the close of that college term, which would be in the middle of the ensuing summer. So I was for sixteen months in all a student in St. Vincent's College.

Most of the students were the sons of French

planters of Louisiana, and the institution was more French than English. Things were ordered very much as they are in the religious houses of Europe. We slept in large dormitories, and ate in a refectory, some one reading aloud the while from an English or French book. The College had its own tailors and shoemakers; and by the favor of the president, who seemed to take a great liking to me, my credit was made good for anything I wanted, and I was provided for as well as the richest of them.

The instructors were all priests, and generally good men. They never required me to change my religion, or to conform more than externally to their worship. I applied myself so zealously to study that, at the expiration of my sixteen months, I was nearly prepared to enter Kenyon College, in which I spent the next four years.

The president of St. Vincent's, Father Stephen V. Ryan, has since met the recognition which his piety and abilities so justly deserved. He is now the venerable Roman Catholic Bishop of Buffalo; and it is with no little pride that I still class him among my most valued and constant friends.

When I came to leave St. Vincent's I drew out a deposit which I had in a bank in Toledo, and gave it into the hands of the College treasurer, reserving for myself only what I thought would be enough to take me back to Ohio.

As good luck would have it, the little steamer Banjo, a show-boat belonging to Dr. Spaulding, the manager of the Floating Palace, was advertised to be at Cape Girardeau the week in which I purposed to leave there. Seeing the names of some of my old comrades on the bills, I waited to meet them. They generously made me bring my trunk on board, and have a free ride to St. Louis, or, if I chose, to Alton, where I was to take the cars for Chicago.

The remembrance of this trip up the river with these jovial, reckless souls has made it my duty always to defend my old associates when I hear the censure heaped on them by inconsiderate ignorance or blind prejudice. And I can take my final leave of the show business and of show people in no better way, I think, than in relating an incident which occurred on this little steamer.

On the afternoon before our arrival at Alton, as I was sitting on the deck by the side of one of the performers, Mr. Edwin Davis, who had been a member of our company on the Floating Palace, he asked me to let him see my money, adding that I might have had imposed upon me some of the "wild-cat" bills then afloat.   Taking out all I had, I placed it in his hands.   He counted it, and scrutinized it thoroughly, and, folding it up carefully, returned it to me with the remark that my bills were all good.

I had no occasion to use my money till I came to pay my railway fare at Alton, when I discovered that my wealth had increased by nearly half.   He had, indeed, been a better judge than myself of my necessities; for, with his generous addition, I had barely enough to take me to my destination.

I met Mr. Davis in New York, years afterward, and offered him the sum he had added to mine, but could not prevail upon him to take it.   And this is the way he stated his reason: "No; it does not belong to me.   Keep it you, till you see some poor fellow as much in need of it as you were then on the Mississippi, and give it to him."

BOOK III.

THE TOUR OF EUROPE FOR $181 IN
CURRENCY.

Æt. 20-22.

CHAPTER I.

I CANNOT tell when the idea of going abroad first came into my mind, but, in a little journal kept in my thirteenth year while travelling with the minstrels, I find the fact that I was going to Europe alluded to as a matter of which there was not the shadow of a doubt.

There is a jolly sort of beggar in San Francisco who says hope is worth twenty-five dollars a month. It must be that I shared with him his principal income during the four years of college life which almost immediately succeeded my wanderings as a minstrel, and which launched me again on the world at twenty. What else besides the hope of Continental travel sustained me during those four years I cannot now say. My pecuniary resources for that whole period were so small that they have tapered entirely out of my remembrance.

Leaving college, I had served, I recollect, but a few months in the post-office of Toledo, Ohio, when I took a deliberate account of my savings one morning, and was gratified.   I found in my possession too large a sum to permit of deferring the realization of my long-cherished dream another day.

Counting my money over and over, I could make no less of it than one hundred and eighty-one dollars, in new United States treasury-notes; and I resigned "mine office," not with the heart-broken feeling of Richelieu, in the play, but still, like him, with the lingering cares of Europe on my mind.

Not the smallest fraction of this vast sum, I had resolved, should be squandered on the ephemeral railroads of our younger civilization.   My treasury-notes were to be dedicated, green, votive offerings, on the older shrines of our race. But the city of Toledo is situated about seven hundred miles from the sea, and it now became an interesting question how this distance was to be compassed for — nothing.

To a good-natured friend of mine in one of

the railroad offices I explained, at considerable length, and with no lack, I flatter myself, of boyish eloquence, the great advantage that would accrue to me from a residence in Europe which the liberality of the companies, in the matter of furnishing passes, would tend to prolong.

I think he became my convert, for he came to me, several hours afterward, with a long face, and gave me to understand that the railroad officials were in the habit of building no dreams of æsthetics that were not founded on a ground-plan of dollars and cents.

At this I became — I do not know which to say — desperately vindictive or vindictively desperate. Anyway, the unfeeling conduct of those corporations induced, then and there, a state of mind which led me into an adventure the least calculated, probably, of any in this history to establish my claims as a moral hero. The next morning I brought my trunk down to the depot and had it checked through to New York. The rules seem not to have been so strictly observed then as they are now. The baggage-master in this instance, at least, taking for granted that I had already secured my ticket, did not ask me to show it; and I was at liberty to stroll about the station all day, listlessly.

Just before dusk a cattle-train arrived from the West and brought with it a lucky thought. I scanned the faces of the drovers till I found one that looked benevolent, and the owner of it I engaged in conversation. He was going on East with his cattle the next morning, and I made a plain statement of my case to him. When I had done, he patted me on the back in such a cordial and stalwart manner, that — as soon as I could get my breath — I took it all as a good augury. And so it was.

I wish I could reproduce more of the dialogue which took place between this honest Westerner and myself, at that first interview. Some of it, at least, I never shall forget, it impressed me as so extraordinary at the time. I can, however, convey no idea of the contrast between his mild kindly face and his harsh bovine voice. It may help you to a kind of silhouette view of the situation, if you will take the pains to imagine the frequent excursions of my puzzled attention from his face to his voice, during the scene which immediately followed.

He had given me to understand that he had eight car-loads of live stock, and that he was entitled to a drover's pass for every four car-loads. Then he suddenly paused, thrust both hands into the pockets of his long-skirted coat, and, feeling about in those spacious alcoves for a silent moment as if in search of something, he asked, in an abrupt bass which seemed to issue from the depths of the coat-tails themselves, —

"How air you — on cattle?"

That was before the days of Mr. Bergh and his excellent society; but, having consulted the speaker's benevolent face and not his voice, as the last authority on the meaning of his question, I answered that I was very kind to cattle as a general thing.

That, he assured me, was not exactly what he meant; he wanted to know whether I had ever done any "droving." On my intimating that, although I had not had much experience, I was perfectly willing to be of service, "Never mind, never mind," he said; "but can you play cards?"

"No," was my ingenuous reply.

"Now that's bad," and he scratched his head vigorously. "Can you smoke, then?"

"A little," faltered I.

My new-made friend seemed much pleased by this response, and continued, —

"All right; you jist git a lot of clay pipes and some tobaccy, and I'll git you a pass!"

As I was turning in utter bewilderment to have his strange prescription filled, "I say, look a here," he said; "take off all that nice harness, or you can't pass for no cattle-man! I'll lend you some old clothes and a pair of big boots. These stock conductors is right peert, they air. You'll have to smoke a heap, and lay around careless in the caboose, or they'll find you out."

The next morning I took my seat in what he called the "caboose," — a sort of passenger-car at the end of the train. When we had been under way about an hour, the burden of my own conscience, or of my friend's boots, or the contemplation of my unsightly disguise, or the amount of tobacco I had smoked, made me deathly sick, — which, on the whole, was rather a fortunate circumstance. It explained to the conductor why I did not get out at the way-stations to tend my cattle, and it also enabled me to hide my face from the conductor, to whom I happened to be known.

I found, as most boys do, that I could smoke better the farther I got from home. What with stopping to let our cattle rest and other delays, it took us nearly a week to reach New York; but before three days had passed I could perform the astonishing feat of putting my friend's boots out of the car window, and of smoking serenely the while, without touching my pipe with my hands.

All the hotels at which we stopped along the route seemed, like the crèmeries of Paris, to exult in the importance of a *spécialité;* and that was that they were supported almost entirely by drovers, and assumed, without a single exception that I can call to mind, the device and title of " The Bull's Head."

There was a smack of old times in the homely comforts as well as in the moderate charges of these quiet taverns. My expenses on the whole journey from Toledo to the sea were, if I recollect aright, a little over three dollars.

CHAPTER II.

TAKING TO EUROPEAN WAYS.

AT New York I found that I should be obliged to pay 130 for exchange on my money. This I did, after buying a through third-class ticket to London for thirty-three dollars in currency.

My memories of a steerage passage across the Atlantic are rather vivid than agreeable. Among all my fellow-passengers in that unsavory precinct I found only one philosopher. He was a British officer who took a third-class ticket that he might spend the difference between that and a cabin fare for English porter, which he imbibed from morning to night. He announced as his firm belief, after much observation upon the high cheek-bones of our countrymen, that the Americans in a few years would degenerate to Indians, — the natural human types of this continent.

It was during the World's Fair that I arrived in London. My whole life there might be writ-

ten down under the general title of " The Adventures of a Straw Hat," for the one which I wore
was the signal for all the sharpers of that great
city to practise their arts upon me.   They took
me for some country youth come up to see the
Exhibition, and the number of skittle-alleys and
thief dens into which they enticed me was, to say
the least, remarkable.

Through the friendly advice of a police detec-
tive, I was finally prevailed upon to purchase a
new English hat, and with this, as a sort of ægis,
I passed out of the British dominions, without
being robbed, — and, indeed, without much of
which to be robbed.

At Paris I witnessed the magnificent *fêtes* of
the Emperor, and took the third-class cars for
Strasbourg and Heidelberg.   At this latter city,
with a sum equal to nearly eighty dollars in gold,
I proposed for an indefinite series of years, to
become a student of the far-famed Karl-Rupert
University.

I was not happy in Heidelberg, therefore, till I
had experienced the mystery of academic matriculation.   All I can recall of that long ceremony
now is, that I had the honor of shaking hands —

sancte dataque dextra pollicitus est is the language in which my diploma speaks of me, commemorating, I believe, that impressive moment — over my passport with a large-moustached German official ; and that I furthermore had the privilege of paying a fee of eleven guldens and twenty-six kreutzers, — a little over four and a half dollars.

After much search and many unintelligible appeals in bad German, through wellnigh every dingy street of Heidelberg, I finally secured a room for two guldens — eighty cents — a month : and such a room! It was on the story next to the clouds. It seemed to be cut into the high gable of the gray old German house by some freak or afterthought of the architect. It was reached by interminable staircases and through a long hall, or passage-way, whose unplastered walls were hung with the rubbish of many generations. It was just large enough to permit of my turning round, after furnishing nooks and corners for a bed, bookcase, wash-stand, and small, semicircular table ; but all was neat and clean, for my room was subject, like the rest of the German world, to the regular Saturday's inundation of soap and water.

Directly opposite, on the other side of the narrow street, but far, far below, was the shop of a sausage-maker. If I had been an enthusiast in mechanics, I should have found much consolation in this fact, as well as a great deal "to lead hope on"; because a sausage-maker's apprentice is really, if not perpetual motion itself, a strong inductive argument in favor of its future discovery. The one to whom I have alluded kept up a continual hacking, day and night, week-day and Sunday. The sound of his meat-axe met my ears the first thing in the morning and the last thing at night; it was, in fact, my matin and my angelus bell.

But, by a principle of compensation, which is one of the kindliest things in nature, this little nook had advantages of which prouder apartments could not boast. I never had, before or since, a room in which I could apply myself to study so assiduously or with so great a zest. It seemed to be haunted with the great spirits of those who have trimmed their lamps in garrets and left the world better for their toils.

This may have been a boyish hallucination, but I shall always believe that the most glorious view of the famous Heidelberg castle, the Molkenkur, and the lofty peak of the Kaiserstuhl, is to be had from the one narrow window of my aerial niche in the dark German gable.

The old castle frowned down upon me from the brow of the mountain just above my head; and often of an evening have I leaned upon my little window-sill, and gazed up at its ruined battlements and ivy-mantled towers. As they grew dimmer and grayer in the waning light, the rents and seams of centuries disappeared, and the palace of the old Electors used to stand before me in its ancient pride.

It may not be generally known that the day-laborer of America has better food and more of it than many a wealthy burgher of Central Europe. Only the very few, in Germany, can indulge in beefsteaks for breakfast. I soon learned to conform myself to the cup of coffee and piece of dry bread of the German's morning repast.

But as I became better acquainted, and gradually more impecunious, I left the *café* where I had before partaken of these luxuries, and betook myself to a baker's shop, where a breakfast of the same kind was furnished me, in company with market-women and others, for four kreutzers, —

about three cents. If I could sometimes have wished for a more liberal allowance of sugar in my coffee, in this humble refectory, I never could complain of a lack of sweetness in the morning gossip of the baker's red-cheeked daughter.

The search for the very cheapest place to get my dinner was not the work of one day, or unattended with some difficulty and much skirmishing. I bethought myself of my sausage-making friend across the way. Indeed, it was a long while before I became so used to the *staccato* music of his meat-axe as to keep from thinking of him most of the time. Engaged as he was in the active production of food, he must certainly, I argued, know something of cheap dinners. I therefore made a descent on the meat-shop one day.

No notice whatever was taken of my knock ; so, pushing the door open, I stood before a dwarfed, long-aproned, pale-faced boy, who turned his hungry eyes upon me, but did not cease his hacking. I launched forth in the kind — I may say, the peculiar kind — of colloquial German I had learned in my three weeks' sojourn in his country.

After I had talked some time, the boy, giving no
rest to his meat-axe, but every once in a while
looking furtively over his shoulder, asked, —

"Do you want any *Wurst?*"

"Sausage ?   No, no."

And I began again, in my original German, and
explained at greater length that I was in search
of a place to get a cheap dinner.   The boy laid
down his meat-axe, eyed me a few seconds in awful silence, then glanced apprehensively over his
shoulder, took up his meat-axe again, and went to
work more lustily than ever.

There was this much about it : either the boy
was deaf, or we stood somewhat in the relation
of the two English girls in Hood's story, — he
could speak German and did not understand
it, and I could understand German and not speak
it.   Still, rather pleased than otherwise at such a
chance to air my newly acquired speech, and on
the whole not a little gratified with my quick
mastery of the language, I began in a higher key,
and, approaching nearer and nearer, demanded in
the sausage-maker's ear whether he knew of a
place to get a cheap dinner.

Down went the meat-axe again, and, with eyes

and mouth wide open, the boy stood speechless before me.

Thus we were both inanely staring at each other when the back door flew open, and a burly lump of tumid humanity stumbled through it with a curse, wanting to know why the boy was not at work. The poor apprentice caught up his cleaver again, and I faced the man who had just entered.

" Do you want any Wurst ? " he asked.

" No, no." And I went over the whole story once more with such perspicuity as shipwrecked patience would naturally inspire in a person thoroughly at sea in a language. In the thick of my oration I detected a cloudy gleam of intelligence spreading itself over the red face of my hearer. My eloquence had touched him at last. I had not quite reached my peroration when —

" *Doch !* " interrupted my fat friend, as he pulled me briskly to the door. " You see that shop, three houses farther down the street ? "

" Yes," said I.

" You are sure you see the right one ? "

"Yes, yes."

" Well, you go right down there. There is a

Frenchman down there. His wife is from Italy. I think, maybe, he can understand the Russian language : *I* can't !"

It was at that moment, I think, I learned to make the distinction between the degrees of benefit one derives from a book-knowledge of a language : it may help you to understand others, but it can hardly be said to help others to understand you.

While on this subject I may be pardoned, I hope, for telling of the more expeditious way I adopted to acquire the other modern tongues, which my subsequent poverty rather than any extraordinary ambition induced me to learn, in order to preserve the disguise of which I shall tell you presently.

On going into an unfamiliar country for the first time, I shut myself up in some cheap garret, with a grammar, for a couple of weeks. Then I sallied forth with a pocket-dictionary, and captured some worthless young fellow without friends or employment. To this luckless person I cleaved without mercy. I followed him — if I could not make him follow me — everywhere,

and talked at him and made him talk. I argued
with him over his three sous' worth of chocolate,
if we were in France, or over his boiled beans
and olive-oil, if we were in Italy.

I asked him questions about everything, if we
walked together in the streets ; and, by the way,
is it not truly wonderful how much one has to
say when he has a difficulty in saying it ? You
may have noticed that a man who stutters, or has
a hair-lip, is always talking. He who learns a
new language is invariably troubled with the
same fruitful suggestiveness, and often, too, with
a more distressful execution.

If, therefore, the patience of my friendless
tutor would sometimes flag, I would attempt to
make him understand my glowing accounts of
the comparative wealth of such vagrants as he
was in my own prosperous, poor man's country,
advising him to immigrate. This occasionally
would have the effect of restoring him to a feeble
interest in life.

But if he would still persist in his low spirits,
and find himself on the verge of asking me why
I did not myself go back to my Eldorado of good-
for-nothings, where he, no doubt, heartily wished

me, then, at that last critical stage of his gloom, I would soothe and cheer him with a penny cigar. Generally speaking, this will not fail thoroughly to overcome your Old World vagabond. He will talk, and even listen, after that. The only difficulty is to know just when to administer to him the cigar: he must not be pampered or spoiled by undue indulgence and luxury.

At first, when I commenced my experiments on these unfortunate beings, and I could see them wince under my laceration of their helpless mother-tongue, I had slight qualms of conscience. Learning to quiet these at last, however, I fastened myself on the most intelligent vagrant at hand, with an almost faultless pre-calculation of my man, and subjected him to my tortures with a triumphant sense of virtue in the act, far transcending, I fancy, that experienced by your enthusiastic *savant* when substantiating some pet theory on a living criminal.

Nothing, I am sure, ever before impressed me so highly with the modest merit that may lie concealed in vagrancy. It would be positively surprising to any one who has not enjoyed the advantage of this desperate method of mastering the colloquial speech of a country, if I should tell how soon I was enabled by it to drop my humble tutor, and, moving out of his neighborhood to some other city in the same state, to utilize and practise upon more pretending persons, in a higher grade of society.

II   P

CHAPTER III.

B UT I must get back to Heidelberg, where the sympathetic reader will not, I trust, have imagined that I went all this time without dinners because the search for one which should be the *ultima Thule* of cheapness was embarrassing and adventurous. I found a place, at last, where a homely abundant midday meal was furnished me in a private family, for one gulden and twenty-six kreutzers per week, — a fraction over eight cents a day. My supper I took at a *Gasthaus*, in company with some theological students, at the cost of about four cents.

Many of my countrymen, who have spent large sums in endeavoring to live cheaply in the same city, will of course believe nothing of this. They have paid dearly for the privilege of being Americans. They date their experiences from hotels supplied with waiters who speak our language, and have dealt at shops on whose windows they have seen blazoned in golden letters, "ENGLISH SPOKEN." They have, in reality, paid the teacher who taught these waiters and those shop-keepers to murder our own vernacular.

By matriculating at the great University of Heidelberg, I became endowed with all the time-honored privileges of students. I could not be arrested or taken through the streets, if I had been guilty of an ordinary crime; I could not be confined in a common prison or go to a common hospital, the University having those institutions for its own particular benefit.

And poverty seemed there to have lost its curse. The very fact of my being a student put me on a social scale above that of the wealthy merchant. This, however, may have been only in the estimation of the collegians themselves.

A fellow-student thought some of going to America, and propounded the following question: "But when I arrive, I shall not have any money, and I shall know nothing of the language of the country; what shall I do?"

"Go to work!" said I.

"What? manual labor! I am too aristo-
cratic!"

That young man, let me add, was then living
on an income of one hundred and ten dollars a
year.

The German student must have his pipe, his
beer, and a life of pleasure at whatever sacrifice.
If he is rich, he pays some attention to his personal appearance. You will see him adorned with
boots of immense length ; *corps* caps and ribbons ;
the number of his duels scored on his red face in
ungainly sword-scars ; and followed by a retinue
of sinecurists, in the shape of great ugly worthless dogs. *His* life is a continued sacrifice to the
merry gods. He is rarely seen at lectures.

Indeed, there is one society or club at the University, the first article of whose constitution
reads, " No member shall at any time, or on
any pretence whatever, after matriculation, be
seen in the University building."

On the other hand, if the student is poor, he
pays very slight attention to what he wears. He
does not the less, however, devote a great portion
of his time to beer, tobacco, and the pursuit

of pleasure. You will see him at the most fre-
quented beer-houses every night. If you go to the
opera, you will observe him also stalking thither,
shiveringly, through the wind, his tight pantaloons
striking his crane-like legs about midships between his feet and knees, and his shoulders
shrugged up in the vain attempt to get more
warmth out of an extremely short coat. He looks
more like the impersonation of Famine, striding
about among men, than the good, honest-hearted
fellow that he is.

For with all his faults, as our more Puritanical
education may lead us to call them, the German
student *is* an honest, generous, noble-hearted
fellow. He sees beyond the smoke of his own
pipe, and has deeper thoughts than those inspired
by beer. His heart swells beyond the bounds
of his petty state. His sympathies are as broad
as the old German Empire.

It is too true, perhaps, that when, in maturer
manhood, he becomes *angestellt* in some life-office
in the gift of his little prince, his liberalism slumbers or dies out ; but that does not affect the
sincerity of his youthful sentiment. I am sure
that I never spoke with one of them, on the sub-

ject, who had not some dream of a great united Germany.

There was no more interested watcher of our late civil strife than the German student. He felt that the battle then waging for the right of self-government had a connection with his hopes for the future of his own severed land. Germany's wrongs and the sigh for universal liberty are the burden of his many songs. No higher and no more appropriate eulogy on the German student can be pronounced than to say that, in his university days at least, he is true to the spirit of one of his most beautiful and most popular melodies, "To the bold deed, the free word, the generous action, woman's love, and the fatherland."

By the laws of German universities, a matriculated student is not obliged to pay for more than the lectures of one professor during a semester, — that is, six months. I managed, therefore, to pay for the cheapest, and attended as many more as I liked ; so about ten dollars a year were my collegiate expenses.

To confess the truth, my calendar and that of

the University did not always agree. I often took
vacations in session time, in the shape of long excursions on foot, and sometimes disappeared from
Heidelberg for weeks together. My *Hausfrau* —
she that received the princely income of eighty
cents a month for my room — at first showed
symptoms of anxiety about me; but she soon
learned to be surprised at no wild freak of her
aerial lodger.

By these tours on foot, — the only philosophical way of travelling, — and by the occasional aid
of the cheap third-class cars of that country,
I visited all parts of Germany, and learned more
of the language, character, and habits of its
odd, warm-souled people than I ever could have
learned at the great hotels and in the first-class
railway carriages. During the long vacations, and
especially after leaving Heidelberg altogether, I
extended my explorations into remoter parts, —
into the Tyrol, Switzerland, Italy, and France.

I travelled in a way in which probably no
American has ever travelled before or since,
namely, disguised as a Handwerksbursche, — a
wandering tradesman. Any one who has been
in Europe will not ask why a stranger in that

land should need to pass himself off as a poor native, if he wants to save money. On the Continent, as a general rule, a man in broadcloth, not personally known to the shop or hotel keeper, pays two prices; whereas a person speaking English, even if clad in fustian, pays three prices; and I should like to see him help himself. The English language has come to be mistaken for a gold-mine all through Europe.

These wandering tradesmen, these Handwerksburschen, let me say, — for they are unknown to nations under free, constitutional governments, — are a sort of fossil remains of feudalism. They are young fellows, half journeymen, half apprentices, who are obliged to wander for two or three years from city to city, working at their trades. They finally return to their homes, weary and poor; having learned little but the rough side of the world, — to make what is called their " masterpiece." If this pass muster, they are entitled to style themselves masters of their trades.

They grow out of that old illiberal principle which compels the son to follow in the footsteps of his father and his grandfather. Yet, for all the narrow-minded enactments and regulations to crush their spirit and make them miserable, they always walk on the sunny side of nature. They are a jovial set of vagabonds, who have rarely the chance to be dishonest, if they had the inclination.

Disguised in the blouse of their class, — something like our Western "warmus," except that it is of thin blue stuff, — I have spent many a happy hour, toiling along the same road with them, listening to their stories and merry songs. If I meet one of them on the highway, he stops, offers me his hand, and exchanges a kindly word. He takes out his pipe, asks me to fill mine from his tobacco-pouch, and tells me all he knows of the road passed over.

He never lodges in a city, unless he has work there. The village inn is his castle; here he obtains his bed at night and his breakfast in the morning for seven kreutzers, — not quite five cents ; and trudges on, smoking and singing, through all Europe. This is the Handwerks-bursche, poor, but merry ; the knight-errant of the bundle and staff; the troubadour and min-nesinger of the nineteenth century.

11 *

In Switzerland, for instance, where almost every one travels as a pedestrian, and where hundreds of our countrymen every year blister their inexperienced feet at the rates of from ten to thirty francs a day, I have journeyed sumptuously — thanks to my disguise — for thirty sous. When addressed in French, if my broken speech was noticed, it was supposed that I was from one of the German cantons; and, in the same manner, if my bad German was detected, I was set down as from one of the French cantons.

This gratuitous naturalization on one day and expatriation on the next had no bad effect whatever on my health, whereas it had the best possible result on my purse.

My blouse was a protection, not only to the respectable suit of clothes which I wore under it, but against all the impositions practised upon travellers. When I arrived at a large city or watering-place, I generally hired a little room for a week, found a cheap place to get my meals, and, after settling prices for everything in advance, divested myself of my disguise, and "did" the galleries and promenades, to the accompaniment of kid gloves and immaculate linen.

But the glory of pedestrianism is not in cities ; it is in the broad highway, on the banks of mighty rivers, or in the narrow footpath winding over mountains. There is such pleasure and pride in the consciousness that one can go where and when one will, without waiting on coaches or trains. Thirty, forty, or fifty good miles left behind in one day, by the means of locomotion nature has given to every one, are not only a consolation to sleep upon at a village inn, but make the sleep sounder and sweeter. I defy any man not to be proud of his strength, when he finds — as almost every one will, after a little practice — that he can make thirty miles on foot, day after day, with perfect ease.

It is, however, just to state that village inns are not always paradises. The hostess sometimes has more lodgers in her beds than she receives money for ; but a practised eye generally detects such places at a glance, and rarely exposes the body to their perils. Every village has at least one respectable inn. Before my personal history had taught me this wisdom by excruciating example, I had good reason to believe that the tortures of the Vehmgericht, the old secret tri-

bunal of Germany, were not the things of the
past which the world thought them. I had
frequent occasion, too, for what might be called
an equanimity of stomach.

I arrived one evening, for instance, at a small
desolate village in the remote eastern part of Ba-
varia, near the Austrian border. I was weary and
hungry, but before mine host of the inn would
have anything to do with me, he sent me on a
wild chase through innumerable narrow, crooked
alleys, in search of the burgomaster to deliver my
passport into his hands and obtain his gracious
permission to remain over night in the place.

The entrance to the mansion of that dignitary
was through a cattle-yard. He had probably
never before in his life heard of the language of
my passport, but that did not prevent his looking
at it with an official air of infinite wisdom. I
returned to the inn at last, fortified with the
requisite credentials.

The hostess now appeared, and asked me what
I would eat, addressing me familiarly in the second person singular. Her long lank frame was
attired in the abominable costume of the Bavarian
peasantry. I could compare her to nothing but

a giant specimen of the Hungarian heron, which I need hardly say is not a pretty bird.

The same room served as parlor and kitchen. I sat patiently and watched her kindling the fire in the great earthen stove, indulging my mind as hungry people are wont to do, with rich visions of imaginary banquets. What was my horror to see her take the eggs, which I had ordered, break them one by one into her greasy leathern apron, and commence beating them vigorously with a pewter spoon !

As soon as I recovered my presence of mind, I considered the folly of remonstrating with her, and, with a great effort, I mildly remarked that she had misunderstood me ; I wanted my eggs boiled. By this stratagem, I preserved my disguise and achieved a cleanly meal in defiance of the leathern apron.

CHAPTER IV.

A FIGHT WITH FAMINE.

IN the mean time, the condition of my finances was becoming hourly more desperate. I had written to innumerable American newspapers, offering to produce a letter a day for five dollars a week, and making all sorts of struggling tenders of brain-work, from which, as a general rule, I heard nothing at all.

At last Christmas came, and found me back at Heidelberg, utterly penniless; over five thousand miles from home, in a country where for a stranger to obtain work was simply hopeless; since the boys in that densely populated land have to pay for the privilege of learning to carry bundles, — a pursuit which is there for three years a necessary introduction to becoming a salesman of the smallest wares. To obtain a situation as beggar was still more hopeless, the competition of native dwarfs and cripples being altogether too powerful for an able-bodied alien.

So here was the end of my one hundred and eighty-one dollars in currency. I had made what is called the tour of Europe; and I now had the prospect of immediate starvation for my pains.

And yet that Christmas day was, by all odds, the happiest day of my life. For, just at fifteen minutes past eleven o'clock, A. M., the postman knocked at the door and handed me very unexpectedly a letter, containing about twenty-five dollars in our money. It came from an American paper, to which I had written, at least, twenty letters for publication, and twenty-five letters asking for money; so it was undoubtedly the twenty-five dunning letters that were paid for. And I shall never be so rich or happy again.

So much has been written about the holidays in Germany, that I cannot be expected to say anything new on the subject. It may, however, have been forgotten by some that the *Weinachten* of the fatherland commence on what we call

"Christmas eve." This is the great night for children. It is their feast. It is the time they have been looking forward to with such wild, glad, gorgeous anticipation. It is the night of the Christmas-tree; and, in all Germany there is no child so poor as not to get something from its green boughs.

Besides this night, Christmas has two whole days, to which respectively there seems to be a logical apportionment of two very important kinds of enjoyment. The first day is assigned to boundless eating, and the second — mildly speaking — to getting drunk; and it is due to the zeal of the Southern Germans, at least, to say that they observe this order of ceremonies with scrupulous exactness.

Now, it may be sentimental, or something worse, but I confess I like to dwell upon the time when twenty-five dollars made me perfectly happy. Memory, you may have observed, has a way of painting frescos with the clouds of distant skies that are even prettier than the lay-figures and life-forms which served for the real models. It was, for instance, a quiet little scene of domestic joy, that Christmas of my student life in Germany; yet, somehow, it has grouped itself in my remembrance, like the masterpiece of Cornelius, the largest fresco of them all.

Frau Hirtel was the domestic little body of whom I rented my airy apartment. Fräulein Anna was her rosy daughter, and this little sunbeam in the house was the only child of the family that I had ever seen; though many and many a time, the name of Karl, the only son and brother, was upon their lips. Karl was a Handwerksbursche, — one of those houseless tradesmen, before dwelt upon; and on this Christmas Karl was expected home from his long, long wanderings.

The illuminated tree on the night before had been laden with many a gift of affectionate remembrance for the absent Karl. As we sat down to the Christmas dinner, there was a vacant place at the table, and in the hearts of the disappointed mother and sister. They could not touch a morsel.

"Are you sure he will come, mamma?" asked the little Anna, after a long silence.

"Yes, my child, unless something has happened; for the way is long from Frankfort, and the poor boy's feet must be sore with his long, long journey."

" What, mamma, if he should n't come ? "

Frau Hirtel's face became very pale, whether at the little Anna's question or at the sudden ringing of the shop-bell, as the door swung open and shut. The next instant Karl was in the middle of the room. His pack and staff fell at his feet, and Frau Hirtel and the Fräulein Anna sprang into his arms.

It was not the merry dinner that succeeded, or the *Glühwein* that made the evening glad, but this one picture which dwells most in my memory. The joy that shone on the careworn and dust-stained face of the returned wanderer, reflected in those of his mother and sister as they stood in that long embrace, has no parallel that I know of in the history of the return of exiled kings.

With my twenty-five dollars I lived cheaper than ever, and for some months longer continued my studies at the University. But one morning I received a letter from the same generous American newspaper, enclosing a draft for fifty dollars, together with a very earnest request that the editor should hear no more from me on any account whatever.

This good fortune was too much for my mental equilibrium. Heidelberg was too small for me. I started the next day for a trip down the Rhine, deck passage.

At Rotterdam I betook myself again to the third-class cars, and occasionally to the bundle and staff. Thus I went through Holland and Belgium, walking leisurely one day over the historic dead of Waterloo.

Arriving finally at Paris, I resolved there to take up my residence. By means of a cheap lodging in the old Latin Quarter, and of a cheaper restaurant on the Boulevard Sevastopol, I managed to subsist for several months.

It was here in Paris that I first met my good friend, George Alfred Townsend, the well-known war-correspondent. To him I was afterward indebted for a short, romantic sketch of my life, in which he says, I believe, among other complimentary things, that the faculty of Heidelberg gave me my tuition for nothing, but that I would not stay with them and study, because I thought it too dear!

But, seriously, I owe Mr. Townsend a real debt of gratitude, for it was he who suggested that I should write an account of certain of my experiences for one of the London magazines. After the questionable success of my multifarious attempts with American newspapers, I trembled at the temerity of the idea. Yet my money was becoming daily and by no means beautifully less. Neither Mr. Townsend nor anybody else but myself was aware that, at the time of his suggestion, my cash capital consisted of one gold napoleon, a silver five-franc piece, and some three or four sous; and even this sum had dwindled considerably before I could muster courage to make the attempt.

At last, in a fit of desperation, I sat down one morning, with the equivalent of about two dollars in my pocket, and commenced my article. In three days more it was on its way to London with an enclosure of British stamps, enough to pay for the letter which should tell me whether it was accepted or rejected.

I shall not dwell longer than I can help upon the painful suspense of the succeeding five or six days; though I do not remember now my grounds for expecting an answer in so short a period.

Up to that time I will venture to say there was not a happier person in the gay capital of France than I had been ; for it is one of the peculiar charms of Paris that it affords abundant amusement for him who spends forty francs a month, as I did, or forty thousand a month, as some do.

I cannot explain now, any more than you can believe in, my happiness then. I know only that the beautiful city was delightful, and that I was delighted. The palaces, the galleries, the gardens, the parks, the music, and the wonderful diorama of the evening Boulevards were free, — as free to me, the vagabond stranger, as they were to the greatest prince ; and I had the additional, though not necessarily comfortable, assurance that I always carried away from them a better appetite for the next meal than did even his inscrutable majesty, the Emperor himself.

But now that I had the growing cares of authorship on my mind, it dwelt more and more upon the waning disks of my franc-pieces, as they swelled for a time illusively into sous, and then tapered into centimes and disappeared from my gaze forever.

At this period I found myself occasionally strolling down to the Seine, and looking over from Pont Neuf at the flood below, swollen with the late rains, and listening to the strange sound it made in the wake of the old stone arches, as it rushed on toward the Morgue, — the famous dead-house, where hundreds of suicides are displayed every year.

Have you ever heard the last " bubbling groan " of a drowning man ? If you have, you will understand the feeling with which, after listening long and steadily to the low rumble of the eddying water, I have received the impression more than once on that old bridge, that I heard the same fatal gurgling sound in the river beneath ; and you will understand the feeling, also, I think, with which, at such times, I cast a hasty glance at the Morgue, not far distant, and hurried on to the more cheerful neighborhood of the garden of the Tuileries.

I would not have you believe that the idea of suicide ever crossed my mind. I merely went and looked into the Seine, on that queer, un-explained principle which impels miserable people, the world over, to haunt wharves and bridges, and to gaze listlessly into water. I have some-times thought, when I saw servant-girls and others out of employ looking, for instance, from the bridge of boats at Manheim into the Rhine, as into the window of an intelligence-office, — I have sometimes thought, I say, that if dogs do go mad from gazing into water, as I think was once believed, they are very miserable dogs, and very much disgusted with the world, before they do it.

One day, — the fourth of my suspense, if I re-member, — when I was more despondent and hungry than usual, I went and looked in through the grating of the Morgue itself. If I had ever had the least thought of throwing myself into the Seine, this horrible sight would have cured me as thoroughly of it as it did of my appetite for the rest of that day.

I feel some diffidence about mentioning a plan — happily abandoned, as you shall see, before put into further execution — which suggested itself to my mind during that hungry week, namely, to visit the Morgue once a day for purposes of economy; but, luckily, I discovered about this time that the smoking of cigarettes made of cheap French tobacco would perform the same service of taking away the appetite, and I adopted the latter more agreeable means to that end.

The fifth and sixth days after sending my article I did scarcely anything but wait about the office for my letter. Finally, a note arrived from Paternoster Row, with just one line of the worst penmanship in it that has ever yet met my eyes; and the painful suspense was only intensified. The writer evidently said something about my article, but what I despaired of making out.

I took the note to my friends, and they were divided about it; some said that the article was rejected, and some that it was accepted. The majority, however, favored the latter opinion, to which, at last, myself was brought, and I was happy.

Not long afterward I received a draft from the publishers for a sum which seemed to me at that time almost fabulous, for the amount of work done. After a hearty meal, and as soon as I had time to think, I considered my fortune made. I was now arrived at the appalling dignity of magazinist, — contributor to the widest-circulated periodical in the language.

I packed my trunk immediately, and started for Italy.

12

CHAPTER V.

I STAYED at Florence all winter, living on the cheapest of food, indeed, but with the very best of company. I haunted the galleries and studios so much that the artists took me for a devotee of art, and never asked me how I lived.

At dusk it was my custom to steal away toward my dinner, passing Michael Angelo's David, forever about to throw the stone across the famous old Piazza, and gliding down a by-street till I came to the market. There, in a little cook-shop, amid the filth and noise of the very raggedest of Florence, I partook of my macaroni, or, if I was fastidious, of my boiled beans and olive-oil, for seven centesimi, — one cent and two fifths of a cent; my bread made of chestnuts for two centesimi, — two fifths of a cent; and my half-glass of wine for seven centesimi,

—my dinner, with a scrap of meat, averaging five cents, and rarely exceeding ten.

My glass of wine may be considered an extravagance. It was not. I could stand the bustle, the uncleanliness, and even the staring at a passably well-dressed person in such an unaccustomed place; but I could not stand the positive amazement expressed by young men and old women, old men and young women, beggars and organ artists, the day when I omitted wine. It was too much for endurance. Public opinion was against me. I pretended to have forgotten to order my wine, and turned off the whole affair with a laugh.

Many and many a time I have seen a poor old creature, who was often my next neighbor at table, pay two centesimi for bread and seven centesimi for wine, and that was her whole meal.

This experience has always helped me to believe the account of that strange incident in the history of the Florentines, given, I think, by Macchiavelli, in which it is related that during the Republican days of Florence, when there was a hostile army making an inroad on their territories, the doughty republicans, having gone out to meet it, lay encamped some time not far from Lucca ; and that, suddenly, when the enemy was almost upon them, they revolted, turned around, and marched home again, to let their territory and the fortunes of their city take care of themselves, because the Florentine army had unfortunately got out of wine !

Sometimes I spent my evenings at the *café*, where I always took my breakfast, and where for three soldi, — three cents, — invested in coffee or chocolate, I could sit as long as I liked, reading the papers, or listening to the talk of my artist friends. It was always cheaper for me to go to the opera — taking a very high seat, by the way — than to have a light and a fire in my room. I have seen an opera with a hundred or more people on the stage at a time, in a theatre as large as, and some say larger than, there is in London or Paris, and all it cost me was eight cents.

Thus I lived on in the city of art and olives. When my money began to give out again, I thought I would condescend to transmit another article to the London magazine which had made my fortune before. I transmitted another article; and at the time when I ought to have heard from it I was reduced to the sum of forty francs.

Receiving, at last, an envelope with the Paternoster mark upon it, I restrained my joy, and opened it leisurely, making merely the mental resolution that I would dine in state that day; for this was a longer article than the first one, and the sum which it would bring must be simply enormous. Then I proceeded to read the following letter : —

"DEAR SIR, — Your article entitled ———— is respectfully declined"!

This time starvation was sure; but I had set my heart on seeing Rome. I thought there would be a sort of melancholy satisfaction in having visited the capital of the ancient world before going to any other new one. I therefore took the next open-topped car for the sea-shore, having previously put my first rough draft of my unfortunate article into a new wrapper, and shipped it off to the editor of a less pretending periodical, published at Edinburgh.

I do not remember how or why, but the night

after I left Florence I had to lie over at Pisa, where I came near being robbed of what little money I had at a miserable, cheap *trattoria*, not far from the famous Leaning Tower. I found a fierce-moustached bandit of a fellow in my room in the middle of the night, stealthily approaching the head of my bed, and scared him away, I shall always believe, by the bad Anglo-Italian in which I expressed my sense of surprise and concern at his untimely and extraordinary conduct.

Two days afterward I took a fourth-class, that is, deck passage on the French steamer, sailing down the Mediterranean from Leghorn. I stayed a week at Rome, and came very near staying much longer. It was, indeed, by a miraculous chance that I ever left the Eternal City. I had not money enough to pay the Pontifical tax on departing travellers.

It is too long a story to tell here, but I slipped through the fingers of the police, and, arriving at Leghorn again, I had not the ten cents to pay the boatman to take me ashore from the steamer.

My trunk, by the way, I had left at Leghorn before starting for Rome ; so that was out of danger, and came properly to hand afterward.

As my lucky star would have it, an American bark was lying at anchor in the bay. It was the first time I had seen the " star-spangled banner " for two years, and I flew to it for protection. I directed the boatman to take me to the American ship.

Standing in the bow of the smaller craft, as soon as she reached the greater one I sprang up the side, and the boatman sprang after me. He detained half of my coat, but I reached the deck, where I kept him at bay with a belaying-pin till some one on the ship was roused ; for it was early in the morning. The ten cents were paid over to the clamorous Italian by a hearty tar, who was moved to see an American in distress, " with his mainsail carried away," — I think that is the way the tar phrased it.

The captain of the ship was a warm-hearted old fellow from down in Maine. He offered to take me home before I asked him. I had a boyish love of independence, and proposed to work. He said he would n't be bothered with me ; he would take me as his only passenger. We settled the matter at last by my contracting grandly to owe him fifty dollars in " greenbacks."

Our vessel was about twenty years old, and laden with rags and great blocks of marble. We had a terrible storm in the Mediterranean, in which we came near going down. The old craft seemed, however, to have some secret understanding with fate; for, having shifted her cargo, she floated, wellnigh on her beam-ends, the rest of that desolate ten weeks through the Mediterranean and across the Atlantic.

I arrived at Boston finally, without a cent. I had directed that all letters should be forwarded from my address at Florence to the care of the merchant to whom our ship was consigned. What was my surprise, then, to be handed by that gentleman an envelope enclosing a draft on London, in pay for the almost-forgotten article which I had sent in sheer desperation, if not in comprehensive revenge, to that Edinburgh magazine!

Greenbacks were then at their heaviest discount, and English exchange at its highest premium. And thus it happened that I sold my draft for American money enough to pay the good-hearted captain and the patriotic tar, and to take me back to Toledo, my starting-place, after an absence of over two years, at the total expense of a little more than three hundred dollars.

Here, at the proper end of my pilgrimage and of this book, while I am figuratively taking off my sandal shoon and hanging up my pilgrim staff, let me say that, although I did not set out with any higher purpose than to tell just such a story as I might tell under oath, still I think I discern in these European adventures what I may term an *ex post facto* moral. Let not the reader, however, practise and amuse his ingenuity by attempting to detect this in the earlier chapters of the present work, or by any manner of means in the pilgrim himself; for, personally, he feels as free from a moral as any pilgrim *he* has ever seen has been free from superfluous linen.

While, therefore, I would not advise any young man to follow directly in my footsteps, yet I hope I have shown that there are means and modes of travel unknown to the guide-books ; that there are cheap ways for the student and man of limited means to see and learn much for little money.

The sight of a sunrise from the Righi is certainly more than compensation for putting up with a poor breakfast.   And the candid traveller, however light his purse, needs never return dyspeptic or misanthropic.   Pure air and hearty exercise in the Alps and on the Danube cannot fail to do him physical good ; while he will find in the human nature with which he comes in contact in every land the sum of the good invariably preponderating over that of the evil.

THE END.

Cambridge : Printed by Welch, Bigelow, and Company.